Preach

By

K.A. Shott

Introduction

It is my distinct pleasure to announce the birth of my fraternal twins, PREACH and IDEAL (a twinning of Didymus).

PREACH and IDEAL relate to each other from their individual and isolated fantasy worldviews but, when taken together, prove synergistic through the mechanical appropriation of Yin Yang.

PREACH is told through the "way of seeing" as a Pentecostal Evangelist.

IDEAL is told through the vision of a Christian Communist.

PREACH | IDEAL (or IDEAL | PREACH if you prefer) are told by characters who have been marginalized, having been designated Fringe, but both—like all zealots—perceive themselves as both misunderstood and persecuted by those they are convinced have misunderstood them.

PREACH will be offered to this sacrificial Time of Change as a PURE INNOCENT—it is generated through trance, faith, conviction, and unfiltered; PREACH is but ONE draft, Alpha and Omega, uncensored and unafraid.

IDEAL will be the offered to this sacrificial Time of Change as PURE VISION—as such it will be my first "Picture" book.

I pray both will serve with Honor and Distinction, Amen to the E. Pluribus Unum we have spectacularly failed to FULFILL; this Time of Treachery will determine if our Failure is a Permanent or Commutable Sentence on the Heart of US A-ll.

Chapter Alpha

"If life *is* short, eat dessert *first*."

A Crone's Wisdom

Day 65:

I pondered God. I studied life. God created life for us to draw understanding of Him. I read the Bible. I contemplated Noah's Ark. I contemplated all other philosophies: every philosophy—those seeking Truth in hope of attaining the Meaning of and to Life will to find a singular truth: Pairs. Everything, without exception, is paired. And so I came to know that Christ was not God's son but his Bride. Christ is the Mother of Earth as it was meant to be his Kingdom. Christ is my Queen, endowed with oppositional but equal power, yet denied access in this world that has fallen into corruption both against its Queen and its King; it is the pairing, the symbiosis, that fulfills the Law Christ established through his human sacrifice of blood—a price that could only be exacted by barbarous and ungodly souls.

~~~

It was the first Wisdom he was given and triggered the first of many occupational transfers.

~~~

Day 64:

And so it begins with the first being last, the last being first, and everything I've ever understood becoming but the footstool of God.

I.   Wisdom of the Sun & the Carousel: As the sun is the center upon which life relies so therefore allow the life we intend to germinate from seed into life through the ways of men not God be but what they are—in Truth: mere imitation. Then, with this humility at not being able to perfect the perfection we corrupt with our arrogant ignorance, we are worthy to attempt to be worthy of caretaking any life, including plants and animals—by first proving, through our actions, that we are worthy within ourselves, proving that we fully submit to the wisdom that has been calling to us for eons. Then, and only then, will we—possibly—be blessed with even a single seed's germination…with the majority of seeds failing even to begin life. For we are not proven worthy caretakers of life for we are not worthy within ourselves; to know if this applies to you, as carefully as you watch your money—as diligently as you care and worry about your account—do as much so for your internal worthiness: how you will know you are unworthy is by how many times you think, speak, or feel that others are not doing as much as you…that is your debt. Pay it off to zero. Then you will begin—begin only—to become worthy of one seed's germination. Become worthier still—ablating the corruption of selfishness and immediate gratification of the self (which includes all you value most such as family, friends, direct spheres of influence)—and you will be entrusted with more seeds…and, eventually, with great, prolonged and sustained effort, one-by-one you will see life from your seeds. Take care then! It is such a wonderful experience—life—that the moment you (through such diligence and discipline) experience the bliss of this…it is very difficult to surrender, to be still…subservient to God, through which the life was entrusted to you and that your great will and effort made you worthy; humans and animals crave. God calls us to be His image—to be more than…to walk on the water…not swim in it. Amen.

~~~

Day 63:

Wisdom of the Great Physician and The Accountant:

Any honest physician will tell you that there is no "warm" to the action of living: you are either living to live or you are living to die.

And only the enlightened Preacher will qualify: "The love of life will not add nor deduct one moment of life from your accounting but Love applied to the Account of Life will mean you die with your ledger in the Black."

~~~

Day 62:

Wisdom of War:

God has been preparing us, training us ALL, from the Beginning until this day for the Final and Determinative war: the Battle Within between Good and Evil.

As with an infant, we have lived—collectively—the External Loci of Control. We have learned the HORROR and NECESSITY of war but we have yet to learn that what we have EXPERIENCED OF WAR has—to date—been CORRUPTION; those with corrupt intent have used WAR for the profit of deceit.

The Lord's voice is simple and there is nothing more beautiful than the TRUTH—which is never bound by words or details until we LASH them together ourselves—which is our exercise of will: which means that we can Un-LASH it and HEAR TRUTH everywhere and in everyone.

We are being called to overcome Babylon. We're being called to set aside our childish way, our reliance on control as an externality, and we're being called to the truth that we are all created warriors for A REASON: to enter the FINAL BATTLEFIELD—our OWN hearts and minds.

To overcome our bondage to the External Loci of Control—to become the Bride of Christ versus the dumb animals lowing in the fields, rutting the soil, or scratching for food—we must exercise Self Discipline and the DESIRE, wholly, to sacrifice the Self for the Greater Purpose prescribed by Christ, the Great Physician—the World Healer—and Bride of God.

In this Battle of the Mind and Heart—as our eons of experience with external war (the model we are meant to model WITHIN OURSELVES) have taught us—we must endure whatever hardships for however long—we must not abandon or surrender our posting—until we achieve total and lasting victory…over OURSELVES>

Through this discipline and through victory of THIS war—which is far more devastatingly painful and full of suffering than all the physical wars of all time combined—we will REALIZE and FULFILL the promise of "A War to End War" which, to now, has failed because Man and Woman, in their hubris of believing THEIR WAY is superior to GOD and CHRIST'S way; the fruit of this marriage (Humanity married to Hubris) is the root of ALL suffering.

Those who now refuse the call to END PHYSICAL WAR by engaging in INTERNAL SELF WAR bring upon them the curse unto three generations; the person who now refuses to go to battle within now will be Patient 0…the curse will then extend from them to their children (both physical and metaphorical…as in their "creations," their produce), to their grandchildren, to their great-grandchildren. For anyone who, knowing now they have the choice and power, to end ALL war…to reduce the suffering in the World of all Brothers and Sisters…it is this willful cruelty that is the curse—it is the cultural transmission, the conditioning, the inheritance—and I am here to testify, to witness, that if this is your choice…that you—for not wanting to die in the trenches of your own mind—would prefer someone else to take your place…I assure you, Sir or Madam, that what you reap will be the most bitter and Strangest Fruit.

Amen.

~~~

Day 61:

A Selfish Wish:

I wish ALL comedians (the most intelligent and most acutely sensitized witnesses of injustice and hypocrisy) would interview, BRUTALLY, anyone who claims to be a religious, philosophical, or hedonistic leader for at least 3 times, each, for at least ONE hour…all televised and PROMOTED HEAVILY.

Comedians like: George Carlin, Billy Connolly, John Stewart, Mel Brooks, Rob Reiner & Son, The Marx Brothers, the Three Stooges, Bing Crosby & Bob Hope…I find it difficult to name, off the top of my head and without thinking, a woman other than Carol Burnett and Lucille

Ball…the women comedians (the women from all professions and callings) make the annals of history in, approximately, a 1:7 ratio compared to men.

This is not the result of MERITOCRATIC measure but the RESULT OF a highly efficient practice of a socially engineered design that has become carefully nuanced and subtle (such is the maturity of Deception—the modern Disruptors use conditioning over pitchforks not because pitchforks proved ineffective but because conditioning proved more efficient).

So the act of contrition for historical lack of inclusion, access, and promotion and IN PUBLIC RECOGNITION of the subscription to both the legislated and the personal practice of a Socially Darwinistic Infrastructure—ALL female comics who wish to, TODAY, must not only be allowed to, UNRESTRAINED AND UNCENSORED, QUESTIONS and the female must go first.

Then, after that first step forward with the female foot…the second step will be that of the male.

Each will get one—equally measured step.

In this attitude, both will, rhythmically and justly, move us forward to a balanced and equitable understanding of Truth.

The Wisdom of SIXTY NINE:

Everyone who's ever enjoyed the number will know is that the most fun comes with intermittent and cooperative turn-taking; the least fun is when both—for whatever motivation—insist on giving AND taking at the same time because…as the Truth seems to reveal…you cannot serve 2 masters…including the giving of and taking of pleasure. But the WORST and TRUST BREAKING 69 is when one, whether in the attitude of giving or taking, chooses their instant and personal gratification—or GREED—over COOPERATIVE PLAY.

The pleasure & fun come from BALANCE whether in numbers or sex: balance is the Wisdom of ALL life's exchanging interaction.

The Wisdom of Two Ears, Two Feet, Two Eyes, and One Mouth:

Two ears: listen more

Two feet: walk, alternately, both worlds of "self" LOVE and "other" LOVE

Two eyes: One eye with correct vision tethered to one eye with faulty vision means HOLISTIC and ACCURATE vision is limited by faulted sight—it is the wise person who, first knowing and then accepting, that the only way to make our way FORWARD through the perilous and UNAVOIDABLE GAUNTLET before us is to have as perfect vision as a FIGHTER PILOT (in other words, perfect by current measurement). In our misunderstanding, we search out ONE person to fly a jet—who has to be perfect (a pressure too great for any human)—but the wisdom of the COPILOT is that no matter how perfect one person's vision may be (perfection is humanly impossible, even the creations we create to be perfect will be imperfect because we begin them already corrupted) the MISSION will be performed CLOSER TO PERFECTION with four imperfect eyes, both sets able to see only half-truths resulting in 1:1 ratio or 50%, than with only TWO EYES (same ratio, same percentage) but more PERFECTED OUTCOME; this is the Paradox of Symbiotic Synergy. With this understanding, then factor in the INTENT ACTION taken WITH THE WISDOM of turn-taking.

The FIRST STEP must be taken by the Women/ the Mothers/ the Brides/ the Sisters/ the Daughters/ the Crones who've been, historically and through social engineering, denied UNFETTERED access to the Public STAGE (aka as having a platform to reach the public in order to make, remake, and make again THEIR argument—with EQUAL promotion and access to the AUDIENCE OF THE PEOPLE) which includes: all people of color, all people with disabilities, all people who are POOR, all people who are STRUGGLING AND SUFFERING (no matter what Tribe they come from…whether rich or poor, people of color or people of non-color, people of ANY faith or people of ANY philosophy—all people who are suffering and struggling must be heard), but especially we must LEND VOICE to all who FEEL they have NOT BEEN HEARD—that's WISDOM.

And then…after coming into a right relationship of—through action with our sight, our feet, our listening…then we can ATTEMPT to master the impossible: a right relationship with ourselves and with others as all relates to OUR TONGUE, our language and desire to find COMMUNITY of like-minded people in order to INDULGE in BIAS—the hardest to overcome, which is why the "training wheels" of our ears, eyes, and feet are meant to "CONDITION" us with the TECHNIQUE of "How" to master what feels unmasterable—which is our mind's HUBRIS…our SLAVEMASTER…because while we are ENSLAVED BY OUR MIND'S CONDITIONING we will be incapable of not only UNDERSTANDING PROPERLY the TRUTH but we will do something FAR WORSE: we will MISLEAD, and this DECEPTION—whether intentional or through misunderstanding and IGNORANCE—will DO HARM…which will CREATE UNECESSARY SUFFERING…and these practices (whether on purpose or by accident—though the suffering resulting from those harmful practices done by accident or through ignorance can atoned for through the acts of contrition OFFERED by those who've been HARMED—the, if a person asks for your shirt…give them your shirt AND jacket—through acts of PROPER CONTRITION with a heart and consciousness actually DESIRING ATONEMENT and the RESTORATION of right RELATIONSHIP not just "do the crime, do the time," or minimal accountability under either legal or moral compulsion because it is the HEART—the DESIRE—that is ESSENTIAL to FORGIVENESS…if the ABUSER is "faking it"…well, men and women, are well versed—at least in sexuality—to know that only one who wants to believe a person's faking is reality will believe the fake is real; but those who want to have a "real" experience will do whatever it takes for the experience to be REAL—for there is no sweeter NECTAR, no sweeter SACRIFICE—as if the burnt fat rising to the Heavens only WE—the HUBRIS of us—is the fat we offer of ourselves to the GREATNESS and for the PLEASURE of us ALL.

This means the most intelligent witnesses MUST battle their OWN SELF FIRST…in order to be WORTHY of the heavy and essential DUTY they bear to help LEAD OUR HUMANITY out of the DARKNESS OF GLOBAL SUFFERING.

It is the only way for the People to Discern Truth…in this time of Deception.

If I had my choice, out of my own Precepts, I'd love to hear Reverend William Barber or anyone from his school of thought or Tribe, be interrogated by the Comedians, so that the People can—with their own hearts and minds—determine if he (or his Tribe) have a part of the Truth…a piece of the puzzle/mosaic/stained glass window…that each person can UTILIZE in their WAR…the pieces of Truth are no different than any other ammunition: to win a physical war it is essential. To win this war, the Truth is the only way to win the Battle Within for the Kingdom of God IS within you and it is your sacred Duty to, as Abraham to Isaac, bring the child in you—the thing you love most…you—to be bother the father who sacrifices and the child being sacrificed—but the story in the Bible is incomplete: where Abraham's order was stayed (like a governor or president's stay of execution) we are not given Pardon: we, as our spiritual self, must carry our child (our ego, our superego, and our id) to the alter before God and we must, in spite of everything crying out for mercy, execute the Self in us…no differently than any other prisoner who receives the death penalty. This death is THE death required to be REBORN, to RESURRECT. We all must commit SELF-SUICIDE OF THE SELF ONLY (not the body)—we must SELF-KILL OF THE SELF ONLY (not the bodies of other living things). God will not accept half measures nor should we EVER desire to offer them to Him. By focusing on others, by focusing on condition (like a hostage negotiator) we are not only revealing our PROFOUND arrogance and ignorance but we are, by refusing to show proper RESPECT and DEFERENCE in every step, every breath, EVERY ACTION, EVERY THOUGHT, and RIGID ADHERENCE TO THE TRUTH THROUGH STOTAN PRACTICE, we are in fact DERELICT IN OUR DUTY TO OUR MASTER, OUR KING, OUR SAVIOR, our God—the Father and the Mother, the husband AND the bride.

I pray that I, unlike Cain, will never again offer anything but the VERY BEST I HAVE TO OFFER to the battle being waged, eons of battle, to establish the WISDOM of God's LOVE and TOLERANCE—to create a "New" Earth—no matter how LOGICAL and RATIONAL it seems…in the world we live in…to continue believing, adhering to, and ministering to what is the OPPOSITION OF CHRIST'S SACRED HEART.

Amen.

[Personal Note: In American Political Practice, Mother's Day needs to be married to (and celebrated) as also "Bill of Rights" Day—for the Bill of Rights men were the Foremothers of our Nation and the micro (the self, literal motherhood) is meant to be a tool of perception to be applied to ever-increasing complexity of organization (ie: Society). This means that, in the U.S., Father's Day needs to be married to "Constitutionalist's" Day for these men represent the Forefathers of our Nation.

The Wisdom of this Truth is that while unequally balanced, the only path forward is one of Destruction—as is true of any "imbalance" in the body, medically speaking.

This is my understanding of the TRUE meaning of the accounted WORDS of God the Father and His Bride, Christ, accessed through the SPIRITUAL GIFT OF DISCERNING POWER bestowed unto me by the power of THE Holy Spirit's Ghost.]

~~~

Day 60:

The following is the making of a vision. It is how the Truth comes to me (perhaps to you as well)—as disparate pieces that, on the surface, appear no differently than a freshly mined diamond: unidentifiable as a thing of value, even if the only value is ascribed versus inherent. I share this with you so that you may see—what I offer you, in terms of wisdom and true understanding, does not come to me as an obvious treasure. It comes to me as material that I must—through slavish labor—agonizingly work…until I find either a nugget of Gold or I am made a Fool.

The following will be told in order from the newest to the oldest—as, spiritually, this is the best, most efficient way, to Truth.

-"Bottom Line: images from veteran comet observer Terry Lovejoy show comet ATLAS - brightening from May 5 to May 9, 2020." Source: Earthsky.org, "Whoa! Comet ATLAS Got Brighter This Week," 5/9/2020 Posted by Deborah Byrd in SPACE| Today's Image.

-"Its nucleus disintegrated and last night I could see three, possibly four, fragments." Source: Gianlucci Maci, Astrophysicist: ATLAS comet broke into pieces on Easter, 04.12.2020. [Personal note: ATLAS first became known to me mid-March—a personal date of importance and a date upon which I travelled to the epicenter of the Covid Pandemic.]; "ATLAS comet 2020 observations show it has a similar orbit to the Great Comet of 1844, which suggests Comet ATLAS may be a fragment of the same 1844 comet." Source: Current News from Astronomy

-2) Searched 1844 Timeline Events: I. "Tanzimât"—internal reference—included initiatives to end the Ottoman SLAVE TRADE—result of large pressure from British government to stop the persecution of CHRISTIANS; II. March 21st, 1844; A) in Bahá'í faith, sublime Porte of the Ottoman Empire submitted a note to the British and French embassies promising to cease EXECUTIONS OF APOSTLES from Islam: Bahá'í referred to this as the "EDICT OF TOLERANCE" (or the stopping of the Muslim execution practice of Jews based on APOSTASY). II. First known ADVENTIST mention of the EDICT by Adventist, William Miller, occurred in 1917; A) "The Edict" prophetic interpretation seen among the religions as SPECIFIC SIGN leading to the FULFILLMENT of PROPHECY" Daniel 8:14/Ezekiel 4:5/Revelation 9:15; B) Edict of Bahá'í 1) 1944: Shoghi Effendi or "God Passes By", 2) 1961: William Sears "Thief in the Night", 3) Religiously, "Hands of the Cause of God,"—Hands considered to have achieved a distinguished rank in service to the religion" 4) There were 50 Hands 5) The title is NO LONGER conferred, 6) The last Hand was Alí Muhammad Varqá (**1911-2007**) [Note: The Wheels always in Motion triggered the 2007 beginning of Global Financial Collapse]; 1844/1845 Timeline for U.S. House of Representatives: 227 total/115 for majority—leader, John Davis (D), Indiana/ minority: Samuel Finley Vinton (Whig), Ohio/ Speaker of the House [Personal note: associated this title with Egyptian burial reference to "Opening of the Mouth"], early leader: Martin van Buren (D)—Andrew Jackson killed van Buren's bid for the 1844 presidency leaving Polk (Tennessee) v. Clay (Kentucky): Polk successfully linked the dispute with England over Oregon and Texas positions on SLAVERY— "The Democratic nominee thus united anti-slavery Northern EXPANSIONISTS who demanded Oregon with the pro-slavery Southern EXPANSIONISTS demanding TEXAS, threatening a sectional split/In national popular vote, Polk beat Clay by FEWER than 40,000 votes…a margin of **1.4%**/ As president, Polk completed American ANNEXATION of Texas, which was the PROXIMATE CAUSE of the MEXICAN-AMERICAN War; III. The Great Comet of 1844 C/1843D1 [Note: as in 2020, 1844 was ALSO A LEAP YEAR]; In the 2020 Leap Year ATLAS comet C/2019Y4 was actually discovered to be crossing MARS' orbit, to come closest to Earth on 5/31/2020 "Sun closer than Mars' Elliptical Orbit" using technique of "AVERTED VISION" [Note: Reference—previous insight from the year of 1896, also a leap year]; 6/6/1844 George Williams (London) sets up 1st YOUTH organization in the WORLD—Young Men's Christian Association; 6/15/1844 Charles Goodyear RECEIVES patent for VULCANIZATION, a process to STRENGTHEN rubber [Note: Mythological Vulcan/Mars references Atlas]; 6/27/1844 JOSEPH SMITH AND HIS BROTHER, Hyrum, are MURDERED in CARTHAGE Jail by ARMED MOB (Carthage, Illinois [Note: Historical interest of Carthage, Punic Wars, and the fall of Hannibal]); 8/28/1844 Frederich ENGLES & Karl MARX meet in Paris, France; 10/22/1844 PREACHER William Miller PREDICTS THE 2nd COMING OF JESUS based on HIS tradition's calculations, leading to the "GREAT DISAPPOINTMENT" which leads to the SECOND GREAT AWAKENING" of Protestant religious revival in the U.S. MAINLY BY PRESBYTERIANS, METHODISTS, and BAPTISTS, which sparked REFORM MOVEMENTS and led to period of ANTEBELLUM SOCIAL REFORM and emphasis on SALVATION BY INSTITUTIONS, leading to the formation of several COLLEGES, SEMINARIES, and MISSION SOCIETIES—this FERVOR BEGAN in Kentucky and Tennessee [Note: current representatives being Speaker of the House, Mitch McConnell (KY) and Rand Paul (TN)]. IV. The 2nd GREAT AWAKENING—new POLITICAL ENTHUSIASM, "While Protestant religions had previously played an important role in American politics, the Second Great Awakening STRENGTHENED the ROLE it would play,"—forming of the Second Party System and Antebellum Reform—"often directly addressing issues of: SLAVERY, GREED, POVERTY—it began PROGRESSIVE MOVEMENTS to REFORM SOCIETY'S ISSUES: alcohol consumption [Note: a too-narrowly defined diagnosis for all the addictions of self-anesthesia that often leads to the path of self-abuse due to biological sensitization syndromes], WOMEN'S RIGHTS, and THE ABOLITION OF SLAVERY/ "Historians stress the common understanding among participants of reform as being PART OF GOD'S PLAN" and "The SPIRIT of EVANGELICAL HUMANITARIAN REFORM was carried on in the ANTEBELLUM WHIG PARTY" [Note: We are now IN NEED of the THIRD GREAT AWAKENING in America (The Trinity fulfilled ONLY by LIVING, CONCIOUSLY and WITH FREE WILL—which means EQUAL ACCESS to ALL TOOLS NEEDED to EXERCISE this "FREED" WILL including but not limited to finance, peace, tranquility, free time to contemplate the greatest challenges of our time with the WISDOM to know that EVERY PERSON, FAITH, and Philosophy has BUT ONE piece of TRUTH to contribute to the world's most complicated algorithm…None can be left behind…as our fates are bound like horses, mules, or dogs hauling heavy loads—The Wisdom of Drivers is to know that the "leader" can't be the most aggressive nor the least but the MOST SENSITIVE to its own team's competing TENSIONS and DRIVES and then—with this UNIQUE understanding—will place the MODERATE but MOST ENLIGHTENED to lead, giving it the AUTHORITY to LEAD, so it can hold back the aggressive nature, which is needed to accomplish Herculean tasks, while accommodating the passive nature, which will…if pulled TOO HARD…simply REFUSE TO MOVE—the WISE DRIVER knows that no matter HOW AGGRESSIVE OR STRONG the "Alpha" is…it CANNOT BEAR FOR LONG to carry DEAD WEIGHT—and this is OUR WORLD'S PARADOX—because the TRUE ALPHA (and Omega) is the Middle Way…this is the Leader needed…the Wise Leader, the Benevolent Leader, the Self-Less and the Enlightened—even if this means we must form a Chimera—Drastic times call for Drastic Measure). In America where Christians are to be KNOWN BY THEIR LOVE, they will be REQUIRED TO DEMONSTRATE—by word and BY DEED—the 2 Commandments of Christ: 1) Love God 2) Love each other.]; IV. ATLAS Comet (2020)/ Ayn Rand "Atlas Shrugged" (1957)—she considered it her "Magnus Opus" which means the title, literally means, "Atlas discarded, disregarded, shed"; Atlas Mythology: Atlas condemned to hold up the CELESTIAL HEAVENS for eternity after TITANOMACHY—the Titan battle between the OLD generation or Titans (Note: we refer to Capitalists with large PROFT as "Titans" in their field/industry) and the NEW generation or OLYMPIANS and their ALLIES who would COME TO REIGN on Mount Olympus—the WAR lasted **10** YEARS [Prophecy Note: 2020 Covid 19 (SarsCov2 in the year of 2019—a novel, Chimeric Virus—results in the FIRST TIME the OLYMPICS is cancelled in "Modern" history.)

This is the process by which these wisdoms are gleaned. It is "nuclear" in terms of the amount of energy it requires, from physical to emotional but especially spiritual. I do not believe most can do this—nor what I would suspect—most would want or CHOOSE to do this…but what NO ONE SHOULD do…is to reject anything achieved through such STOTAN efforts by myself and ALL OTHERS from ALL WALKS and BELIEFS in LIFE. There will always be some TRUTH, some WISDOM, granted to those who—for LOVE of OTHERS MORE THAN SELF—accept the MISSON to TRANSFORM our world into that which GOD envisioned for us and that we—up to now and through our lack of will and personal sacrifice—have so BADLY FAILED to realize. Our most favored GUEST, our King, is coming to visit the MANSIONS HE has given to us (or even as one mansion with MANY ROOMS) …inside of us…and for everyone who's ever cleaned even a small space—let alone not one but MANY ROOMS of ONE MANSION, let alone the MANY ROOMS OF MANY MANSIONS—if we are not spending each and every day preparing the "homes" or "rooms" we've been entrusted with for our Master's return (if we are not spending at MINIMUM the EQUIVALENT time and effort for our SPIRITUAL hygiene and ATTRACTIVENESS as we spend on lotions, powders, haircuts, plastic surgery, physical exercise for aesthetic purposes, thinking of and preparing and purchasing food and cleaning ourselves after all proves waste requiring cleaning or we get sick (and die) from filth and disease…if we are NOT SPENDING SPIRITUAL EQUIVALENCY in whatever philosophy/faith we adhere to…then we are FAILURES! Everyone who has grocery shopped or prepared food knows that often it is the perfect looking fruit…an avocado for example…that "feels" right and "looks" right but after buying it and taking it home—all excited to enjoy it—find that once cut open…is rotten. What good is a gorgeous externality when the inside/internal spirit rots, spreading rot and multiplying rot, until our physical body finally represents our internal "body"—the stench of DEATH. It does not have to be this way—I promise you. The Stotan Method: Equivalency. Or spiritual death. There can be no middle way in our intention. There is EVERY way by which it is achieved. You will know which is "Healthy" by the FRUITS is produces and you will LEARN TO JUDGE those who spread CORRUPTION of the spirit in us ALL. Amen.

~~~

Day 59:

Prophecy upon pondering Daniel 7:

-The first chimera is the Mother/the Bride of Christ who—as a Warrior—accepts that loss of life is the requisite sacrifice in this world of War but the INTENTION of the 1st CHIMERA is to GIVE (to deliver unto) each person that survives the ABILITY, in their MIND, to HEAR the TRUTH! [Note: this is the only Chimera I have the authority to speak of in terms of intention]

-The second chimera is of the Father. It will be—in orders of magnitude—more brutal than the Mother's/the Brides.

-The 3rd & 4th Chimeras are Woman and Man, respectively; we WILL WITNESS the power of SYNERGY for they will have Biblical KNOWLEDGE of each other and will SPAWN HORROR as we've NEVER even had the CREATIVITY to DREAM; the final maturation will, somehow be INDUSTRIAL in NATURE and will be, somehow, the most DESTRUCTIVE of all by a magnitude of 7x70. Selah

~~~

Day 58:

Wisdom of MOVEMENT:

ALL movement offers a piece of HEALING for the BODY; COMPETITION is essential but it must ONLY be self-competition—in relation with others movement must be cooperative; this is the way to kill arrogance and hubris within ourselves. So if you are an OLYMPIAN do not compete against your fellow ATHLETE…only yourself. Help your OPPONENTS to be the BEST THEY CAN BE and if—through your OWN SELF COMPETITION TO IMPROVE— you "win" then give your "WINNING" to the ATHLETE WHO CAME IN LAST. Give them the accolades, the glory, the MONEY, the OPPORTUNITIES…if this is difficult for you then it should be a clear indicator that you struggle with PRIDE AND ATTACHMENT. For why, knowing that your own competition with yourself made you a WINNER, would you NEED ANYTHING MORE? Whereas the person who came in last…their NEED for your HELP is greater than your DESIRE for what will only lure you away from the BATTLEFIELD WITHIN as if a fish drawn to the hook by food.

All Movement, All Sport, All Music, Mimes, Acrobats, Martial Artists, Dancers, Yogi, Weightlifters, Runners, Swimmers—ALL MOVEMENT—is a way to HEAL THE BODY if the INTERNAL BATTLEFIELD is either raging or won but it is HUNTING that OFFERS THE GREATEST OPPORTUNITY for VICTORY IN THIS BATTLE—only this World has misunderstood that the "Animal" to be hunted is not a CREATURE UPON THE EARTH but the CREATURE WITHIN EACH AND EVERY ONE OF US or our "Animal/Primal/Reptilian" Brain/Consciousness or Lack thereof.

In RESPECTFUL HUNTING, the animal killed is cleaned by the HUNTER and ALL OF IT IS CONSUMED—there is NO WASTE because the HUNTER RESPECTS and HONORS the LIFE that was SACRIFICED for the HUNTER'S SURIVAL: many modern hunters have either forgotten the Ancient Ways or, I fear, more have REJECTED THEIR WISDOM.

The Ancient Wisdom of a RESPECTFUL HUNT was meant to be of help us now, now that we have developed the INTELLECT to be ABLE to FULFILL CHRIST'S COMMANDS, TEACHES US TO HUNT our own INTERNAL ANIMAL, to stalk, to be patient, to be determined, to LABOR, to SUFFER (Hunting the Ancient Way is always an exercise in suffering…for the hunter), to FAIL MORE THAN SUCCEED even after SPENDING GREAT PERSONAL EXPENSE, to be JOYFUL and THANKFUL for the SUCCESS, to CAREFULLY PREPARE the carcass/to HARVEST THE FLESH, to HAUL the DEAD'S WEIGHT on one's OWN BACK and through one's WILL and COST in ENERGY. Only then…can the SUSTENANCE be granted.

This is the exact method we must do with our animal selves. The hunting and killing of Self-Animal is EQUALLY REQUIRED of us ALL as Leo Tolstoy correctly understood, "The Kingdom of God IS Within Us."

~~~

Day 57:

I.   The Wisdom of Naming a Ranch by K.A. Shott

I'd name my ranch "Asylum Attempt #1 K" because even though my intention is altruism I am still attached to my hubris and must acknowledge that it is a pressing and present part of me that I can, even though in my instinctual reaction to assert myself, choose to ACT based on the consciousness of the morally correct path of altruism.

II.   The Wisdom of Two Feet

We have 2 feet because we're meant to walk, alternately, one foot in each world (the world of SOLO-self and the world of ALL-self). It is not selfish to do for yourself as long as it is not at the expense or harm to another. It is right and good to care for yourself as you are a being just like ALL beings but our actions (walking, stepping, feet are all part of the physical world of action) must alternate, 1:1 ratio, to do for others FIRST, then for the self SECOND—wash, rinse, repeat. Always beginning with the service of others before self will help create morally right focus. Performing physical acts for others first before self will create right action. Alternating selfless with self will create right internal balance.

It is in this Neutral Zone where the field of Battle for Self can begin.

III.   Wisdom of Biology v. Anthropomorphism

A bull or stag is not defending "his"…he is defending the women, children, elderly, and those injured or sick because he is PROTECTING his FAMILY from a bull/stag who wants to TAKE what is NOT his—and the defending stag/bull—as well as all of his herd family—understand, instinctually, that for their PROTECTOR to fail, to fall in defeat, means that the children, the elderly, and injured and sick will be killed either through direct action or through neglect as the USURPER will make sure HIS progeny takes primacy.

Those with corrupt intent tell us that the intruding bull/stag is only out to spread his seed, that the whole of biology is Darwinism. I agree. It IS all Darwinism. The corruption comes from the INTERPRETATION of what we can, objectively see. The Corruption is that this is NATURAL FOR MAN…that men are no different than bulls or stags or dogs and THAT is where the Deception is applied in order to spread the progeny of Corruption because we—as humans with a conscious mind and made in the IMAGE OF GOD (not beasts)—are meant to watch the ANIMALS, in their unconsciousness and instinctual nature, not to JUSTIFY AND EXCUSE the IMMORALITY OF MANKIND, but to see them as the MIRROR FOR OURSELVES…so we can look, deeply inside, and SEE…what WE ARE DOING that is ANIMAL…and OVERCOME IT. This is the pathway to God, to Enlightenment, to creating a Heaven of the Hell in our minds instead of the Hell of the Heavenly Kingdom of God Within Us.

We walk on TWO feet, one in each world (the self and the other) but we must—with all our MIGHT AND FOCUS—choose not to walk with EITHER FOOT…as an ANIMAL but as MANKIND; this is the path to Humanitarianism.

~~~

Day 56:

The following is the making of a vision.

.0."Bill Murray asked Warren Buffet and the Billionaire gave a Powerful Answer on Income Inequality," by Julia La Roche, Yahoo Finance, 5/5/2020 .1. Questions asked: regarding Covid essential workers (aka low wage, undervalued, no insurance, no retirement, no stockpiles, healthcare [Note: did not differentiate healthcare workers which, as with all institutions and people, is diverse in terms of class and security—a C.N.A. or paramedic is not in the same socio-economic class as a cardiac surgeon but all are grouped less carefully than we address Phylum and Family in Biology; this lack of precision leads to GROSS MISUNDERSTANDING and applies to

ALL OTHER SOCIETAL ISSUES WHERE UNEQUAL ACCESS EXIST SUCH AS THE VARYING DEGREES OF FOOD SAFETY BASED ON SES, INCLUDING BUT NOT LIMITED TO CONSISTENT AND NON-THREATENED ACCESS TO NON-TOXIC WATER AND FOODS AS WELL AS THE EQUAL DISTRIBUTION OF ESSENTIAL SUPPLIES TO ALL.].0. FOR EACH SEEMINGLY "HOMOGENOUS" GROUPING OF ANY PEOPLE THERE ARE CLASS/ACCESS/SES STABILITY-SUSTAINABILITY ISSUES THAT VARY—WILDLY—BASED ON THE GROUP'S CONSTITUENCY. GROUPING, AS CURRENTLY APPLIED, IS NOT REPRESENTATIVE AND THESE UNADDRESSED INEQUALITIES IN ACCESS, GROUPING STATEMENTS THAT OMIT THE TRUTH, FUNCTION AS A DECEPTIVE MECHANISM BY WHICH INEQUALITY NOT ONLY PERSISTS BUT THRIVES.1. WARREN BUFFET STATES THAT THE SOLUTION IS TO INCREASE EARNED INCOME CREDIT TO LOW AND MODERATE INCOME WORKERS AND NOT TO INCREASE MINIMUM WAGE, STATING INCREASE IN MINIMUM WAGE WILL DECREASE JOBS.0. [NOTE: INCREASING BOTH EARNED INCOME CREDIT—WHICH IS DIFFICULT TO QUALIFY FOR AND HAS NARROW PARAMETERS, WHICH MEANS THAT IT IS A BONE THROWN TO A CROWD OF STARVING PEOPLE—AND MINIMUM WAGE WOULD NOT, SIGNIFICANTLY, DECREASE JOBS…BUT IT WOULD LIMIT PROFIT. ALSO, NO ACTUAL "SMALL" BUSINESS SHOULD BE UNAIDED BY "BIG" BUSINESS…IN OTHER WORDS…FROM THOSE WHO CAN TO THOSE WHO CAN'T: IF DOING RIGHT BY WORKERS, THEIR FAMILIES, AND SOCIETY THREATENS THE STABILITY OF SMALL BUSINESSES WITH DESTRUCTION…THEN THOSE WITH THE ABILITY (THE ASSETS AND KNOWLEDGE AND ACCESS TO POWER) TO GIVE—AS THE BIGGER ENTITY—TO THOSE WHO ARE SMALLER AND HAVE GREATEST NEED. WIN/WIN…SMALL BUSINESS STAYS IN BUSINESS THROUGH THE PROPER MARRIAGE TO BIG BUSINESS—BY CHOICE— AND THEN THE WORKERS, ALL, SEE THAT BOTH ARE WORKING TOGETHER—A HEALTHY AND PROPER MARRIAGE—TO BE THE BEST PARENTS/CARETAKERS OF THOSE WHO—LIKE ONE'S OWN CHILDREN—ARE DEPENDENT UPON THEIR SUCCESSFUL MARRIAGE.].1. [NOTE: THOUGH NO ONE ASKED ME, MY SOLUTION TO THE WEALTHY & POWERFUL IS TO TAKE OUT YOUR MAPS, USE YOUR MOST FAVORITE PROPERTY, IT BECOMES THE CENTER POINT, DRAW A CIRCUMFERENCE USING WHAT YOU CHERISH AS THE PLACE TO BEGIN YOUR COMMISSION, DETERMINE A 5-ACRE EQUIVALENCY FROM YOUR UNIQUE POINT. IF IN THE COUNTRY OR LARGE ESTATE, MEASURE IT IN ACREAGE—IF URBAN, MEASURE IT IN FINANCIAL EQUIVALENCY, SO IF YOUR APARTMENT IS IN A LUXURY BUILDING AND IT IS ALL YOU HAVE, SELL IT—YOU KEEP TEN PERCENT OF THE SALE AND GIVE, TO THE POOREST PERSON WITHIN YOUR FIVE ACRE CIRCUMFERENCE THE 90% OF THE PROPERTY YOU SOLD. WHEN YOU'VE DONE THAT…WASH, RINSE, REPEAT, UNTIL YOU HAVE—AT THE MOST--$700,000 TOTAL ASSET IN 2020 AND, IN THE FUTURE, WHATEVER THE FINANCIAL EQUIVALENCY IS (IF PAST IS PRECEDENT THEN $700,000 IN 2020 WILL, IN COLA TERMS, BE A LARGER DOLLAR AMOUNT BUT WORTH LESS IN BUYING POWER—AS ALL WHO ARE POOR CAN ATTEST—HOWEVER, IT IS IMPORTANT THAT WEALTH GENERATORS AND WEALTH INNOVATORS HAVE THE TOOLS NEEDED TO FULFILL THEIR GIFTS AND TALENTS…SO THEY MUST—IN A WORLD OF MONEY AND CAPITAL—HAVE THE TOOLS THEY NEED—MONEY IS BUT A TOOL THAT CAN BE USED FOR GREAT EVIL OR GREATER GOOD—SO THE MONEY GENERATORS ARE AS MUCH A GIFT TO A SOCIETY AS ARE THE ARTISTS…BUT WHAT FRUITS ARE PRODUCED…HOW THE TOOL IS USED…IS WHAT DETERMINES

GOOD V. EVIL. TO DATE, WEALTH AND POWER HAS BEEN OF THE SELF (WITH BONES, LIKE BUFFET'S SUGGESTION IN THIS TIME OF A GLOBAL PANDEMIC AND GLOBAL FINANCIAL COLLAPSE, THROWN TO THE MOST DESPERATE AMONG US—THIS FAILURE TO READ THE TIME, TO DO THE RIGHT THING BECAUSE IT IS THE RIGHT THING TO DO, TO PRACTICE APPEASEMENT IN HOPES OF RETURNING TO "BUSINESS AS USUAL"—THIS IS THE PATH OF DESTRUCTION FOR US ALL…AND THE CREATION, THE BIRTHING OF, HELL IN THE HEAVEN OF OUR MINDS].0. WARREN BUFFET IS NOT A GOOD FAITH ACTOR WHEN HE SAYS, "NOBODY SHOULD GET LEFT BEHIND IN SUCH A WEALTHY NATION." YET THE APPLICATION OF HIS SUGGESTIONS WILL DO NOTHING TO STAUNCH THE BLEEDING OF THE POOR AND SUFFERING BECAUSE IT, AS HAS BEEN HISTORICALLY TRUE, IS TOO LITTLE, TOO LATE, AND LACKS VISION FOR HOW TO LIVE…BECAUSE CORRUPTION OF HOW WE LIVE, HOW WEALTH AND POWER ARE BIRTHED AND CONTINUE TO INHERIT, WILL NOT—UNLESS THE PERSON WIELDING THOSE TOOLS—BECOME VICTORIOUS WITHIN THEMSELVES BY KILLING THEIR INTERNAL "ANIMAL" WHICH INCLUDES, BUT IS NOT LIMITED TO, HUBRIS. IN ORDER FOR THE WEALTHY AND POWERFUL TO DEFEAT THEIR INNER ANIMAL THEY MUST RESPECT FREE WILL BY LISTENING TO WHAT THE POOREST AND LEAST POWERFUL TELL THEM THEY NEED…AND PROVIDE IT. OFFER YOUR VERY BEST AND NOT "BEST" AS IS MOST VALUABLE NECESSARILY BUT WHAT YOU LOVE/VALUE MOST (BE ABEL NOT CAIN) AND LET THEM DECIDE…DO NOT INFLUENCE OR MANIPULATE. IF YOU ARE GENUINE IN YOUR OFFERING IT WILL SAVE YOU—YOU PERSONALLY—FROM FALLING YOU'RE YOUR OWN INTERNAL CHAOS, DARKNESS, AND DESTRUCTION. THE WEALTHY AND POWERFUL ARE BEING CALLED TO OVERCOME THE SIN OF CAIN—IT IS YOUR FREE WILL TO DECIDE WHETHER YOU WILL ANSWER THIS CALL BUT IT IS ONLY YOU WHO CAN…THEREFORE YOUR FAILURE IS THE SUFFERING OF THE WORLD. YOUR FAILURE IS THE DISAPPOINTMENT OF GOD, WHO GAVE US CAIN AND ABEL'S DEATH TO BE INSTRUCTIVE, AND YOUR FAILURE TO "DO UNTO OTHERS AS YOU'D HAVE THEM DO TO YOU," IS THE DISAPPOINTMENT OF CHRIST'S COMMANDS FOR HIS CHRISTIAN SOLDIERS.

~~~

Day 55:

Wisdom

Listening to an MIT anatomist I think:

If only we'd studied—with STOTAN practice—how TO live instead of HOW to live and if we'd studied, intently and with proper support (personally, socially, financially, promotion) how TO die instead of HOW we die, then we would not be in such an unprecedented and degraded state to face the TRIBULATION. Now is the "All Hands on Deck" and this is NOT a drill.

~~~

Day 54:

Inspired by the film, "The Biggest Little Farm," and the book, "Five Acres to Independence," but my vision is this hybridization + a Model of Collective Good=sustainable ecosystem with conscious focus on inner-personal relationship to all externality to be always laboring to be of HELP while, with STOTAN discipline PRACTICE NO HARM. In other words, I envision the INFRASTRUCTURE (the application of the intellectual, emotional, and physical infrastructure) used at BURNING MAN; a place where people come to "Camp" while leaving no "personal" footprint (ecologically or otherwise) other than the memories of interactive relationship—to the land and to each other—while practicing "Radical ACCEPTANCE" (radical TOLERANCE) and where everything is "FREE" but where OFFERINGS OF each person's GIFTS AND TALENTS to the COLLECTIVE GOOD result in most REPORTING the RECEIPT of an irrevocable "TREASURE" in the form of ATTESTING to the BEST of what exists inside each one of us ("The Kingdom of God is Within Us," Leo Tolstoy).

The Estimated Cost of a 5-Acre Self-Sufficiency Farm

Basically developed/established utilizable/fertile land $600,000

The most basic housing per person: 8ft Yurt (Stripper Model) total supply and setup cost $16,000

Handicap access/Ramp $20,000

Land Irrigation $10,000

Land Electricity $10,000

Land Plumbing $10,000

Jersey Cow $1,800 purchase/ initial vet care $1,000/ delivery $1,000/infrastructure $10,000

Laying Chickens $50 purchase/ infrastructure $1,000

Garden (utilizing square foot gardening land & water conservation)

1. Infrastructure & startup supply $30,000
2. Recurring/annual plant/soil/nutrient no less than $1000/growth season
3. Outdoor "Tree" shower (efficient use of clean "grey" water) on each tree $30,000

Multiply Estimate by TWO…because everyone knows that whatever you THINK it will "cost" to do ANYTHING…is always insufficient to the NEEDS of the PROJECT because we can "imagine" and we can "estimate" but we are NOT GOOD PREDICTORS of the CURVE BALL…that always strikes the "innovators" out; prediction—even imaginative ones—cannot factor, with any accuracy, the reality of CHAOS. So the safest thing is to study REALITY, and in this moment, it is, on average, a 1:2 ratio of what we BELIEVE is needed, even as an expert in an area, to what is ACTUALLY needed.

AND THEN ADD TO THIS the need of an annual income of at least $200,000 per annum (at least for 6 of the 7 year cycle of Sabbatical) so as to render unto Caesar, to protect and defend in the Court, and to—after establishing the pump's PRIME—use STOTAN practice to, hopefully and with God's GRACE and through Christ's POWER—maintain what was so hardly fought for, what required the ultimate in the BLOOD & TREASURE of the SELF.

~~~

Day 53

On pondering the Sermon on the Mount (KJV) Matthew 5:23-24

"Therefore if thou bring thy gift to the altar, and rememberest that thy brother hath ought against thee; Leave there thy gift before the altar, and go thy way; FIRST BE RECONCILED TO THY BROTHER, and THEN come and offer thy gift."

[Note: we are ALL brothers and sisters. The Wisdom is that if a person has a grievance ("ought") with another person—RECONCILE FIRST and BEFORE going to the altar. Because you going to the altar is for the SELF—it is your personal relationship with God and your social relationship with your Tribe. We must be more SELF-LESS, more OTHER FOCUSSED, because having right RELATIONSHIP with each other is what CHRIST told us HE desires…by denying others the gift of grievance relief, to place OUR relation to God above OUR relation with each other is to DENY CHRIST'S COMMAND…therefore it is NOT TO LOVE GOD FIRST OR MOST…but to—in our OWN WAY—choose SELF over not only our brothers and sisters…but over God and Christ.]

~~~

Day 52:

Wisdom of Air & Water to the Soul:

The inventor of the barometer describes us (life on Earth) as submersed in air as if we are under "water" but it is the air (represented as water).

Evolutionists describe life ON Earth as emerging/transitioning FROM being submersed in water and transforming into being "submersed" in air.

Wisdom to the Soul: Perhaps what comes next (after our mortality) is being submersed in…_____. It is unknown and unknowable BUT AS REAL AS AIR AND WATER.

~~~

Day 51:

   Grouping, or classification, is a cornerstone to the scientific method. Nothing could be more logical. So if I group two performances requiring the silence of its actors and showed you two performances, that of a mime and that of a ballerina (both conveying stories nonverbally), then asked you to determine the supremacy of one over the other—how could you, objectively?

   I'm suggesting that whichever you choose reveals your preference which is, unequivocally and objectively, the meaning of bias. We, as humans, are not objective or rational by nature but contemplating—with intention and commitment—our individual preferences we can begin to confront our own bias.

   Once I could understand this, conceptually, I also understood that I had to find a way to constrain my Hubris (my Id, Ego, and Superego) if I was to succeed.

   This, then, felt absolutely overwhelming and impossible (having a little experience with athletics…I knew I'd never conditioned at a "pro" level in anything let alone something that felt to me as if the future of life itself depended on my success because I could never be the person who asked of others what I had not accomplished myself).

   This little anxiety experience resulted in an immediate intellectual and emotional withdrawal as if a spinal cord reflex loop pulling my hand from a hot stove before my mind could even recognize there was anything wrong.

   But, as with any reflex (even a subconscious reflex) the moment passed quickly because my rational mind (perhaps also reflexive) recalled the fact that no matter how experienced or disciplined an average professional baseball player is they will, on average, bat roughly 300 and this reality allowed me to afford myself the permission to fail as badly as them, hoping that by applying the wisdom of their Stotan strategy to that of the "mastery of self" I would be able to finally "see" my own bias.

~~~

Day 51:

The Wisdom of the LONG game:

When I was in my late teens, through personal experience and observation, I came to a "truth" which I thought was encapsulated (or a stand-alone truth). I was very excited and proud to have "discovered" what I knew was a "key" to understanding my existence—which, in my youthful ignorance and arrogance (ie Hubris) immediately projected that "my truth" was not only EVERYONE ELSE'S "truth" (even if I, in "my" wisdom could see what everyone else either hadn't yet or couldn't) AND I was thoroughly convinced that if everyone would just accept my newly discovered truth, and it was "applied" to their existence (willfully but sometimes not…as an ignorant person might, with direct experience, REALIZE that what you "offered" was actually of "benefit" so… "the ends are RATIONALIZED as NOBLE (or they are argued as being "justified") as the INTENTION of the MEANS is believed to be ALTRUISTIC…

But this is a poisoned well…for the poison—the flaw from which only suffering can be born—is the arrogance and ignorance (the Hubris) of believing that ANY ONE TRUTH (or method of discovering Truth…which also humbles itself as it is never "discovered" but always in a state of "being" or "becoming" or drawing "closer" to discovery (an example: the worldview of scientific method).

So when I'd discovered a "truth" as a teenager I, as a vessel for that knowledge, was too inexperienced and undisciplined not to swallow the poison pill of the "joy" over discovering what I believed—what I "knew"—was a truth that could help reduce suffering in the world…and through this unskillful—naïve and undisciplined—"interpretation" of a truth…lacking the wisdom I now have as a Crone…that "truth"…though "a" truth remained in my "heart and mind" but in the World…it also remained—ineffectual; the "poison" of my "blindness" (my Hubris) would not allow the truth I'd been entrusted with to bear fruit.

Until now…and now…with the Wisdom of a Crone…while uncovering yet another truth—a qualifier that changes EVERYTHING of what I could possibly have understood of my "original" truth…I will not reveal it to you.

Not because I have a secret—for I'm telling you THE Secret in the reason why—now—I choose NOT to speak what I feel, what I "know" is a Truth…because I'm rejecting the Hubris of MY BELIEF THAT I HAVE FOUND a/any TRUTH!

For if, in my teenage naivety and lack of discipline, I was able to find what many seek but are unable to find (ie Exceptionalism enflames Hubris)…and this led to "a poisoned well" or "a poisoned fruit" but now…as a Crone…I am, wholeheartedly convinced that the "modifier" I now see MUST be applied to THAT ORIGINAL truth for it to actually BE truth…and I acted or "believed" based on the same DESIRE of my youth (to eradicate the unnecessary suffering of all Life on the Earth)…then I would have LEARNED NOTHING!

I will have CHANGED nothing is FOURTY YEARS!

For the "TRUTH" wasn't an idea or, upon further reflection and will, a modification of THAT IDEA…

The Truth, the Whole Truth, and Nothing BUT the TRUTH…is that my DESIRE REQUIRES me to become incapable of, BY CHOICE, of "Believing" that "my" truth "should" be applied to anyone else's Reality.

Once I could accept this, once I'd witnessed the Wisdom of this through applying it to my OWN life…I learned that what I'd "believed" was the or "a" truth…was but a WAY for ME to find the TRUTHFUL PATH FOR ME (and if I desire to "teach" or "spread" "my" worldview…it is that we, all Life on Earth, are—one and the same in that each "Individual" worldview will be where each Life can find their UNIQUE truth—and, then, COLLECTIVELY, we will be ABLE to come together to FINALLY GIVE ME WHAT I HAVE—my whole life—DESIRED.

I HAVE NO GREATER DESIRE THAN: the eradication of unnecessary suffering for ALL LIFE ON THE EARTH.

Until then, the Wisdom comes not from me telling you what I did—or did not—do but rather to ask you to do and not to do what you know (in your "gut" or at the core of your being) what must be done to accomplish whatever YOUR greatest DESIRE is.

From a Christian worldview (based on Red Letters) I pledge my fealty to Christ under the Sigil: "They will know we are Christians by our Love, by our Love, yes they'll KNOW we are CHRISTIANS by our LOVE."

I know this worldview is in Mortal Combat with that of its Identical Twin (its Didymus) and I believe, unlike most of my Tribe, that the outcome of this Battle is yet determined (A world could be filled with war veterans able to differentiate between: mission, "rallying", and Reality).

This Battle is one of Ideology.

This Battle is one for the Soul—not body.

This Battle's Outcome is yet to be determined and I will share one aspect of my "transitional" truth experience: whatever you "believe" is the "outcome" (from whatever worldview perspective and regardless of the depth of your experience) you are, most assuredly and decidedly, WRONG!

I assert this as the actual "Lesson" I was meant to learn: Humiliation for having suffered my own Arrogance and Ignorance, when offered the "opportunity" to repeat my OFFENSE (as tempting as it was and as badly as I have DESIRED…my whole life…for the outcome it FELT like it offered) I CHOSE TO ACT DIFFERENTLY BECAUSE I'D APPLIED DISCIPLINE TO MY MIND (to my "thinking" and "believing"…the twins of Didymus and Christ…the two-sided coin of blessing and curse), and then…having received that "Truth"…I, immediately, fell to the temptation of sharing it with you NOW.

You see…I share this with you not to pontificate, not to "tell" you anything but to "share" with you the struggle—the fight—to describe to you, as carefully as any Queen, the encapsulated BORDERS OF MY BATTLE…so that you, my brothers and sister whom I love, each and every one…will learn this ONE WISDOM: there is no external battle…only the external manifestation of our SOUL'S INTERNAL battle.

If our fruits, our ACTIONS, are not producing—up to THREE CONSECUTIVE GENERATIONS AFTER—what is: good, beautiful, upright, loving, generous, self-sacrificing/altruistic, empathetic, sympathetic or what is NURTURING and EMPOWERING then the fruits produced from FAILURE ARE BITTER FRUITS POISONING THE WORLD for a total of 4 GENERATIONS (the person who fails to produce "good" fruit as well as the person who cultivates "poison" is Person 0…the learned behaviors of poison cultivation or refusal of Duty will, based on sociology and psychology, exert Affect for, on average, three CONSECUTIVE generations…unless one of those "links" in the chain "breaks" the "cycle" of Abuse).

~~~

Day 50:

Wisdom of EthicWork

It is ESSENTIAL that WORK be meaningful to the WORKER. It is VITAL for the worker's work to be MEANINGFUL. It is CRITICAL that the INFRASTRUCTURE of WORK be built on the FOUNDATION OF RESPECT FOR THE WORKER'S NEED for MEANING IN WORK, which means that EMPLOYERS are REQUIRED to ASK: "Are you, MY employee, RECEIVING MEANING from your work FOR ME?"

AND

The Employer MUST LISTEN AND ACT/REACT to the worker's HONEST ANSWER.

If the worker says, "yes," then the employer—out of their own PERSONAL GROWTH as nurtured by self-driven CURIOSITY—should ask, "What about your WORK gives MEANING to you?"

The employer then, out of CURIOSITY—and in the spirit of RESPECT—will LISTEN…and ask more questions (because when one stops asking questions it is rarely because they're sufficiently educated or informed but because they've either grown bored or are not, in fact, interested—this is a good "dashboard indicator light" for those entrusted with power…if you're not listening…FIGURE OUT WHY…and know that it will, 99% of the time, be about YOU, not the "other").

But if the employer, after asking the worker, is told that the work is NOT meaningful to the worker (ie it is work done to "pay" to "live") then the employer KNOWS the worker is not LIVING WHILE WORKING (for the LIFE of Humans DEPENDS on MEANING); all employers who do not BOTHER to even ASK if the WORK they're exchanging for MONEY with their employees is adding ONE IOTA of LIFE to the worker's livelihood…they are SHOWING US (all of us) THEIR heart—whether it is one of respectful consideration for ALL life or if THEIRS is the HEART of SELF.

~~~

Day 50:

The Wisdom of "No Grievance"

In my personal journey through interpersonal relationship I realized that I'd been "keeping score" of all the "wrong." It was an unconscious/subconscious attempt to "make the case" with "evidence" (overwhelming at that) to "prove" to those who were "wronging" me that THEIR behavior was 1) hurtful/damaging 2) "their" choice and 3) a "consistent/repeating" PATTERN.

This led to a MIND consumed.

First came frustration for try as I might to make "my" case—having to keep a running tally of "facts"—I realized that what I'd thought was "ignorance" (therefore I had to "enlighten"_ wasn't ignorance at all (because unless there is some form of cognitive damage, even a person with cognitive insufficiency can learn…if they are "enlightened" with the frequency and intensity with which I approached my interpersonal relationship) which meant facing a HARD TRUTH: that what injured me didn't injure them.

What ripped my heart out—was innocuous to them. Even if they could do a thought experiment, an empathy experiment, the fact that—in THEIR WORLDVIEW—the action, the inaction would NEVER be felt BY THEM as pain or suffering PREVENTED THEM (as if a prophylactic) from "feeling" the pain their ACTION/INACTION delivered to me.

This is BIAS.

I understood then that BIAS could not be changed from the outside-in because ALL BIAS IS SELF-INTEREST and as long as a person is MOTIVATED TOWARDS SELF, in that state of "selfishness," an external attempt to CHANGE BIAS will only EVER BE the school teacher's voice in Charlie Brown: a sound that is understood to "be" language but has no "meaning."

LIFE requires MEANING; Death of Life is Meaninglessness.

I learned, then, the Wisdom of the Serenity Prayer: "God grant me the serenity to accept the things I cannot change, the COURAGE to change what I can, the WISDOM to know the difference."

I had to accept that what I love (people, Life) would not stop HARMING as long as it SERVED THEIR SELF-INTEREST.

And that no matter "how much" they loved me—truly LOVED—they would never, NEVER love me or anything external to them MORE than they LOVED THEMSELVES until THEY DECIDED TO.

Our external world is a reflection of the ugliness, the suffering, the corruption of our INTERNAL world.

This was not an easy lesson for me. For I love everyone. I have lived what loving that way FEELS like—and I have derived GREAT MEANING from the sacrificing of SELF.

So now when a devastatingly painful experience occurs, I feel it. I grieve it. I express it knowing my "education" will not change what the receiver does not WANT to change but expressing it because it is the TRUTH OF ME…and I believe—wholeheartedly—in the Truth, the WHOLE truth, and NOTHING but the Truth… and then I have to accept that they WILL hurt me, in exactly the SAME WAY, most likely until the day our lives cease.

I accept them—that they are lost in themselves—and that this is painful to external life…but not nearly as painful as it is to THEM in their INTERNAL LIFE (even if they are unaware/unconscious of it)…for wherever they turn for meaning, for pleasure, for comfort—as long as they serve the SELF over the OTHER—the "benefit" will be as if Fentanyl (or any addiction) in that "sensitization" will occur (it will take more and more to feel less and less unto death).

To know this is to grieve *that* death—the millions of deaths in ONE PERSON'S SINGLE LIFE—the Mortem of each failed (resisted) opportunity to evolve into the loving, peaceful, and tranquil beings we were intended to be BY NOW.

So I sit now with MORE COLLECTIVE pain for knowing these truths…but more PERSONAL PEACE because I discovered ONE TOOL that helped me that I will share with you (with the caveat that it most likely will NOT work for you, but it might so, in my feeling, it is worth sharing):

When I get hurt or angry or "triggered" or "riled up"…I say, to myself, "No Grievance."

This isn't discounting the merit of my grievance nor is it excusing the aggrieved behavior; it is giving myself permission to, while accepting MY OWN AUTHORITY TO EVALUATE AND REPORT, say, decidedly, "That is UNACCEPTABLE," and, thus informed, the HONUS OF RESPONSIBILITY is THEN PLACED UPON the person who has behave egregiously.

I realized that I am meant to be a WITNESS not GOD.

It is not my place to change anyone but myself. It is not my place to expect, as a human, of others what I am not able to do myself. And while I STILL FAIL…I have NO AUTHORITY to tell ANYONE HOW TO LIVE…

BUT I DO—with EVERY AUTHORITY and OBLIGATION—to bear WITNESS, TRUTHFULLY.

What others do, when faced with a Truth they cannot, personally, relate to or can cognitively or emotionally empathize with, is NOT MY PLACE TO CONSIDER.

What is my PLACE? The place that believes in the PROMISE of a New Earth…and that there is A WAY…though obfuscated and sabotaged…and that way to what COULD be…begins by exploring the UNIVERSE OUTSIDE OF YOURSELF…the galaxy of your SELF…and learning that you are an intricate PART but you are not THE part and neither is your worldview (or mine).

~~~

Day 49:

Noble Desire functions, *in* the Self, as Craving without the Practice of Noble Self as Primacy

My life's desire has been—as long as I can recall desiring—what I, as a child, called "world peace" but have come to name as, "Eradication of unnecessary and discretionable suffering."

But I have learned that this Desire is but ONE (though the one I'm most attached to) of MANY and I MUST overcome THIS desire…and that this (the one I'm most attached to and that "feels" impossible to achieve no differently than the feats of all Hero Journeys) but the FIRST STEP on the path.

This is both overwhelming and liberating. Overwhelming because it feels impossible to surrender my longing for what I know is of good to ALL but liberating because I now know that my Goal (to "eradicate" unnecessary suffering) IS being met, one step at a time by ONE PERSON at a time…my misunderstanding was that of SCALE and THAT misunderstanding was a source of suffering for ME. If I can reduce my suffering, I—as a cell in the Organism of US— will "reduce" our collective suffering…but the only way to SCALE UP to the degree REQUIRED in order to realize my Desire…is for EVERYONE to "reduce" collective suffering…cell by cell…until we are—holistically healed.

Until then—if ever—I will have to be serene in the confidence of knowing that I have done all I, alone, can in order to achieve a Noble Intention.

~~~

Day 48:

The Wisdom of the Order of Operations

The evolution of my personal "order of operations" when no "prescribed" order was offered.

1) As a child: the power of Agape love and acceptance
2) As a young woman: the power of sex

3) As a married woman: the power of submission and discipline
4) As a naïve in faith: the power of naivety and vulnerability
5) As an athlete: the power of proper and accurate assessment and evaluation (judgment)
6) As an intellectual: the power of humility (for it was here I learned that ALL I could EVER "know"—with BEST EFFORT and BEST PRACTICES—was ALWAYS LIMITED (or tainted) by what I did NOT (would or could not also) "know."

~~~

Day 47:

A Wisdom Deceived (the case for and against Law Enforcement):

The wisdom: "Tell the truth, the whole truth, and nothing but the truth."

The Biblical wisdom of that wisdom: you can't serve two masters

The Original Sin of Law Enforcement: legal "loophole"

The Fruit of that original sin is evident in Law Enforcement's Current Credo: "Trust BUT verify."

Deception cannot, for long, endure the scrutiny of Reality's Truth for if one's "desire" is to "verify"…the DESIRE ITSELF IS ANTITHETICAL TO TRUST…and one CAN'T serve two masters.

If one is not practicing TRUST by desiring TRUST instead of "verification."

Because everyone knows, "Practice makes perfect," so perhaps we're meant to be "trusting" each other (in spite of PERSONAL SUFFERING FROM EVERY DECEPTION WE ENDURE) because, by practicing trust in spite of vulnerability to the pain when that trust is betrayed, we IMPROVE OUR SKILL IN TRUSTING.

So that when we're faced with TRUSTING something GREATER, we'll be in the PROPER CONDITION (like a professional athlete) to ATTEMPT the TASK ASKED.

For Abrahamic faiths—it will take a lifetime of practice between our THREE TRIBES before we can BEGIN TO ATTEMPT the NOBLE PRACTICE of "trusting God with all your heart, first and MOST;" what I'm saying, is ALL OF US in Abrahamic faith that have not MASTERED OUR OWN DESIRE…are FAILING and our "coach" is evaluating our performance, as we speak—we MUST IMPROVE OUR PERFORMANCE!

The FIRST STEP for the Abrahamics: trust—even when that trust is violated—as MANY TIMES as you HOPE GOD GRANTS YOU the "GRACE" you "feel" you've ALREADY SECURED.

~~~

Day 46:

Wisdom of Apologetics

    I.   Physics: "'When a gravitational wave is traveling, it sees the curvature of spacetime, including the energy that was generated by the gravitational waves produced in the past.' Berti says. The first stone you drop into a calm pond sends out smooth ripples across the surface. If you drop another stone immediately after, the surface is no longer smooth—leftover ripples from the previous stone will interfere with new ripples from the second one. Gravitational waves work similarly, but the medium is spacetime itself, not water." Livescience.com, "General Relativity Passes the Ratio's Test," by Daniel Garisto 5/26/2020

               If, "A rose is a rose is a rose" (by any other name a rose is still a rose) is true then perhaps a wave, a stream, and a soul might be but Rose.

    II.   Biology: Resurrection Life Forms teach us that the seed/essence of Life can lie dormant for so long that—from the outside—it is believed lifeless. Historically, the majority of people (including scientists) while using their own powers of observation could only view lack of life as Death but some scientists believed differently and, through advances in objective scientific methodology, have been able to prove that there are LifeForms that, while seeming to be dead, Live. we've seen, objectively, for

~~~

Day 45:

The Enigma to Decipher what is, and is not, Personal Bias

In an act of contrition I will make the attempt to, objectively, "decode" whatever message might be presenting after subtracting my Desire (eradication of unnecessary and discretionable suffering for all Life on Earth) from its equation. Once the Preacher has been fully expressed while respecting the Stotan method of self-discipline and intellectual curiosity, I will search and remove all references to "you" from the whole document. Though I can speak to the part of "we" and "us" that includes "me"…I have no authority or right to speak to whatever part you do or do not play in the Whole of Life.

So gone will be: should, must, all, only, need other than that of first or third person or the collective form of second person (or "us").

~~~

Day 44:

Wisdom of the UNANSWERED

On 2020.05.18 I searched in Google: "Black man killed…"

The autofil "suggested" possible "endings" to what I had yet fully expressed (like a romantic partner finishing "my" sentences because they "know" me so well).

The autofil's suggested endings were"

…in_____

…in_____

…in _____

…in_____

And the listing of all the "individual" black men who'd been killed filled page after page, year after year.

I was searching for the black man who'd been publically executed while physically subdued by police officers through a version of public lynching (if you define lynching as hanging only and not all the torture that, typically, accompanied the hanging and if you define "hanging" forensically as asphyxiation because the cause of death from a ballistic hanging that breaks the spine/neck is literally/technically asphyxiation].

There are so man "black man killed" that even "breaking news" of things like RIOTS…that one black human death (man or woman) simply doesn't CARRY ENOUGH WEIGHT to come out "on top" of the FEED. [Note: Feed also refers to grain fed to livestock, including chickens; chickens "scratch" which also refers to $.]

It is quickly buried, a mass grave, beneath "pressing" news…like Riots and Looting…without what seems to be a GENUINE INTEREST in addressing the UNDERLYING ROOT of rioting (chronic oppression) or looting (chronic poverty) all while those in positions of "authority"— which is the double-sided coin of REPONSIBILITY—"prescribe" to the INJURED the prescription that EASES the AUTHORITY'S discomfort or woe: how about treating the "PATIENT" FIRST, not by what YOU think THEY need (to do or not to do) but, like a GOOD FAITH DOCTOR, take a COMPLETE PATIENT HISTORY to note SYMPTOMS but a doctor can't PRESCRIBE ANYTHING without an ACCURTE DIAGNOSES!

Last time I checked, for my doctor to accurately diagnose me he/she has to:

1) Trust that I'm a) telling them the truth to the best of my knowledge b) that I want to improve my own health c) that I will do MY part to heal d) EXPECTING them to do THEIR PART ETHICALLY and to the BEST of their ABILITY
2) Actually spend time talking to me and ASKING questions THEY WANT TO HEAR…because the GOAL is CHANGE (if sick, get better—if better, maintain better for as long as possible…knowing that, eventually, even the "better" get sick).
3) That the doctor will UTILIZE EVERY ASSET AVAILABLE to them to EASE THE PAIN AND SUFFERING OF THE PATIENTS that EXPECT them to, responsibly, ADMINISTER.

The Call: Since I was not present to the public lynching of George Floyd by four law enforcement officers, what can I do?

Answer: thought experiment.

My George Floyd THOUGT EXPERIMENT:

I imagine what I hope I WOULD do for this is the HEART OF MY CONSCIENCE (even if my truest DESIRE FOR WHAT IS GOOD and RIGHT is defeated, in reality, by the "creature" of me). Because if I can't even imagine doing the right thing, how can I "actually" do the right thing?

But, as with all experiments, every variable must be considered and in this reenactment there are four primary actors: George Floyd (the murdered), the Murderer, the Accomplices, and the Observers.

Day 43 (is Day 42 continued):

Wisdom of Dogs, Horses, and Christian "Attitude"

Being raised on a farm I learned animal.

I learned that even an aggressive dog would not, usually, attack me if I whimpered and assumed a submissive posture—as if I were a puppy—when they attacked. Not always. For I learned, in animal, that there were aggressive animals who, by nature or because of fear, attacked regardless of my "attitude."

I had to accept this Truth in order to be a ABLE to give my consent—the consent in the above scenario is that I, upon knowing the dog is going to attack me and knowing that even if I assume the "correct" attitude there is still probably a 70% chance that the dog will attack me anyways, I then CHOOSE what I will do.

I can run. I can fight. I can perform the action I know works only 30% of the time, accepting the Reality of what WILL happen to me…70% of the time.

Only I can decide this…for me…and me alone.

Bravery is a word like God. It is not meant to be spoken glibly, casually, lightly. It requires reverence, sobriety, and solemnity…and it doesn't belong—nor can it be possessed by 70% of humans who, like the dogs above, out of fear or nature, will attack those who are in "correct attitude."

Horses (and cattle) offer different wisdom for they are, by nature, unwilling to tread on anything that isn't SOLID GROUND.

Horses (cattle, and most animals) can be "trained" often through a combination of utilizing carrot/stick conditioning and through route behavior conditioning.

But—no differently than the dog—30% of horses will be unable…no matter how brutal the stick or sweet the grain…to TREAD UPON a BODY. It goes against their nature and the fact that another "creature" (a human with consciousness) can "condition" an animal to directly contradict its own nature…to "make" it do what it, in its BEING, is REPULSED BY…I believe is the very definition of ABUSE.

That said, the protestor who lies on the ground before charging horses can take courage knowing that only 70% of them—because of the ABUSE THEY'D SUFFERED—will actually TRAMPLE them. This means the protestor has a 30% chance of being unharmed.

This requires the protestor to engage in a Risk/Benefit analysis and, as with CONSENT and BRAVERY, only I can decide this…for me…and me alone: why do we judge each other's "bravery" when, as if horse and dog, the statistical reality is that the MAJORITY OF US WILL FAIL THIS TEST—so perhaps we should judge not our "outcome" but our "indefatigable attempt."

The Christian Attitude: a thought experiment (history would prove this approach unsuccessful but history, predominantly, is written by the wealthy so perhaps both what it upholds as success and condemns as defeat reflect bias more than Reality).

I imagine myself at the Protest. I feel the anxiety, the adrenaline. I feel my heart racing, I'm sweating, my mouth is dry, I can't see as broadly but my focus is clear. I see what's coming. The banging shields—the sound makes my heart beat to "their" rhythm—and the cadence of their marching feet bring to my mind a litany of the images I'd learned from History…I know the intent is intimidation—I know because I once wore that uniform.

I know that the hearts of my brothers and sisters wearing them are also beating, driven by the Hortator of their own baton's cadence upon the shield they bear. I know that 30% of them will develop PTSD from what they're about to do.

I know that a percentage of the 30% whose conscience screams, "Don't!" will. I know that their suffering after will be unbearable.

I look at the wall of humans in "costume" hoping that the role they're "playing" no differently than ANY ACTOR (and that the carrots or avoidance of sticks) will be reward enough to offset the suffering that ALWAYS OCCURS when a person betrays their own conscience.

So before they even march towards me…my heart breaks for that 30% but especially so for the percentage of that 30% who do it anyway—for their suffering will be the GREATEST for it is INTERNAL and of the SELF.

As for the percentage of the 30% who HONOR their conscience and REFUSE—their suffering will also be GREAT because the 70% of those by their side who are fully conditioned (either by route training and incentive or by natural tendency) will attack ALL WHO FAIL TO ATTACK—however, for the percentage of the 30% who will be attacked by their own compatriots no differently than the "oppositional brother and sister" for REFUSING TO VIOLATE THEIR OWN CONSCIENCE…yes, they will suffer—but only EXTERNALLY.

The difference between external and internal suffering is the difference between the Power of the Moon as compared to that of the Sun; LIFE (and suffering in Life) is about scale or Ratio.

So now, with moral empathy towards my brothers and sisters (towards all the "creatures" including the Chargers, the dogs, and humans) and after performing my personal risk/benefit analysis, knowing that—overwhelmingly—the odds mean that I will exit this conflict badly injured…or dead, and accepting that I am most likely to fail at being Brave but I will not stop attempting to BE brave, I—in my Thought Experiment—accept the challenge of THIS "reality."

One can't be a professional baseball player without thousands of hours of practice—why should we expect the mastering of bravery to be any different?

I accept the Reality of the conditions I'm facing and the most likely outcome but there is one more thing I must contend with before I can engage: the brothers and sisters who mean to do "harm."

As with being a child on the farm studying creatures (horses and dogs) to discover the proper "attitude" with which to approach their aggressiveness, I must consider my fellow brother/sister-creatures.

If a dog's dogdom results from its dog nature and a horse's horsedom results from its horse nature, than a human's kingdom means what with regard to its NATURE?

America has long claimed its Divine "Right" of Kings through David (ironically) but as with the words, "God," and "Bravery," a name is not only to be "benefitted" from (blessing) but to be "accountable for" (can also be a blessing but because of rebellion is, historically speaking, almost always a curse) and the TITLE the American's have SELF-IDENTIFIED with is: Christian. No differently than the nature of a horse or dog, the Christian also has a "nature" and, in conflict they will have to make a CHOICE.

So when facing the police Charger I will lay, prostrate on the ground, before their hooves—knowing that 70% of them will trample me.

When facing the police Dog I will lay, prostrate on the ground, whimpering and crying like a puppy—knowing 70% of them will mangle me.

When facing a Christian Nation's Police/Military I will strip naked, fall to my knees, close my eyes, and FOCUS MY WHOLE HEART AND MIND on what is the GREATEST OF ALL

RIGHTEOUSNESS (and the UNIVERSE THIS ENCOMPASSES)—knowing that 70% will ABUSE ME…even unto prison and death (like Jesus).

I will kneel, naked and ceaselessly praying until either I am abused or I am passed by but I will NOT be "moved."

1) Nakedness is important—for like the whining puppy—it addresses GENESIS in a GODLY attitude for what are clothes but our "Creature" comfort after SINNING AGAINST GOD? So Christians must FACE GOD—and each other, especially in conflict—naked, physically, with the hope of "overcoming" the original sin that resulted in SEPERATION FROM GOD; in other words, as a Christian I choose MY PERSONAL discomfort/suffering (for being naked in public has GOT to be not only terrifyingly vulnerable but also DAMNED EMBARRASSING AND HUMILIATING…ask Jesus) but, in ACTION, I am placing my Christian VALUES above my own "creature" comfort and NO Christian can argue against this motivation.

2) On my knees—for like the charging horse or cow—kneeling (religious prostration) is at the CORE of the Christian soul; they will have to OVERCOME THEIR OWN SOUL in order to ABUSE a naked Christian in an attitude of PRAYER.

3) Hand folded—in a time of violence escalation and justification—hands folded in prayer from a naked Christian in an ATTITUDE OF PRAYER—will never hold up in a Christian court as being perceived, by the abusing officer, as "life threatening," for if an officer "fears for his/her life" when faced with folded hands in prayer—then there goes "freedom of religion" in America, translated as "Christian."

These three things I am now doing in my mind.

I have a sticker on my computer that reads, "There is nothing in the world that can trouble you as much as your own thoughts." I loved it the moment I saw it not because I believed it true (there are plenty of things in Reality that are more troubling than what my mind can imagine, as it can only imagine what it's learned and experienced and I've led a relatively sheltered life so my mind is limited in its imaginations, troubling or otherwise) but because it placed POWER in REALM of the MIND. I'd always done thought experiments but this gave me the COURAGE I needed to ACCEPT THEIR POWER.

In my mind I begin to strip off my clothes, carefully and ritualistically, for in this Act of Contrition I am communing with God—I am begging Him to Restore a Right Relationship within me by acknowledging that I—Eve—was the one who, of my own FREE WILL, was the one who'd pulled away…who withdrew…who "preferred" to comfort myself by assuaging my self-consciousness with that first "robe" and now I must remove it, by choice, and BEG for God to accept my nakedness as a TOKEN of my DESIRE for Reconciliation.

Piece by piece I will remove my clothing, folding it neatly—with great respect and appreciation for all the comfort they've given me…even though that comfort was also a source of sorrow for being "separated" from God—and I will stack, each item, atop the other (as an elephant atop an elephant ad infinitum) until there is NO MORE. Then I will place them on the ground and they will, for the LAST

TIME, act as a barrier—no longer between me|self and God but between the HARSH WORLD and my SOFT FLESH.

I will not, however, remove the Joan of Arc pendant (the canonized patron saint of Soldiers) from around my neck; it is my "noose of CHOICE" for it does not hang there to comfort me or to lend me strength—it hangs as a condemnation.

The Saint around my neck has become the Albatross (Cooleridge's "Rhime"). It testifies against me: for all I have failed to do in thought, word, and deed to ACCURATELY REPRESENT MY KING'S HEART, by what I have done and by what I have left UNDONE (I pray for God's mercy; my failures are in the order of magnitude of 70x7 to the 3rd degree of ALL of Paul's denials).

And now, naked all but for the SYMBOL OF PERSONAL FAILURE, I put MY KNEE on the NECK of what is the REAL THREAT TO ME: that which separates me from God (my shame as represented by clothing) and hope that my ACT of REJECTING this FIRST WRONG is an acceptable sacrifice to God.

People laugh at my nakedness—jeering and recording so that my humiliation can be replayed for the benefit of others—I'm a Crone after all.

I accept this humiliation, willingly and gladly, for I know that I "believe" what I am protesting is WORTH LOSING PRIDE.

In my mind I see the line approaching. I close my eyes even though the "creature" in me, the focus that comes from adrenaline, will—like "Clockwork Orange"—pry my lids open…I, in my STRENGTH OF WILL…FORCE THEM CLOSED. I know, in my mind, that I "believe" what I am protesting in WORTH EXERCISING FAITH.

In my mind I HEAR. The feet, the shields, the horse's hooves (a sound I've deeply loved as a child on a farm but have come to associate with the Sound of War and Oppression). I feel my own heart's beating synchronize in "the" rhythm that "triggers" the release of ADRENALINE (something I am already drowning in from being humiliated and willingly blinded)…the surging endorphin makes the internal reality of me its own BATTLEFIELD…but I will not ABANDON MY POST even if it means that my nerves are on FIRE!

I will not open my eyes. I will not speak. The Kingdom of God IS WITHIN ME…and He—my Father, my King, my Husband…He is with me and I feel the adrenaline ease—the soothing BALM of the Holy Spirit—and I feel my eyelids begin to relax…not that they will fail to remain CLOSED but because with God's strength (he is my Yoke-Mate) I do not have to LABOR to do what is RIGHT BY GOD.

I will pray from my knees, unceasingly, for GOD'S strength to fortify me to be able to suffer as HONORABLY and PEACEFULLY as Thich Quang Duc did on June 11, 1969 in Vietnam; in my faith I do not believe in my own strength (of mind, body, or spirit) so unlike the Buddhist I must face this suffering without being able to self-soothe—the ability for me to suffer in order to Honor the WILL of my Prince of Peace depends on God's will ALONE.

Now the men and women are upon me. I am knocked about. I am kicked. I am beaten. I am trodden upon. I am arrested, not in small part BECAUSE OF MY NAKEDNESS.

But I am unafraid and I am VICTORIOUS because I am, in all my ACTIONS, FAITHFULLY HONORING the CHRISTIAN GOD! My conscience is clean. I will not suffer INTERNALLY in spite of whatever I suffer in my external body.

I cannot say the same for the American Christian Nation. For how can one face such a "Reflection" and believe it beautiful? If America can do this, they are no different than the queen from "Snow White and the Seven Dwarves" for only an "evil creature" can look into a mirror and fail to see its own monstrosity.

How can a Christian Nation look at a faithful sister naked in the street (in the Tradition of David's nakedness in HONOR of God), in an attitude of ceaseless prayer for the nation (a nation claiming the Providence of CHRIST to, finally, ACT and FULFILL the TWO COMMANDS OF CHRIST: love God first/MOST & love EACH OTHER (not just your own Tribe) as Jesus loves YOU), and say, "She is a Criminal (an immoral anarchist, anti-fascist, communist traitor who is an unpatriotic heathen/whore"?

As if a drone from the sky and able to take in the "larger scale" of the imagery above.

Remember Kim Phuc? Kim Phuc was the terrified young girl from the iconic Vietnam War photo who'd suffered severe burns after being bombed with Napalm by US troops in 1972.

Sometimes the POWER of ONE…can CHANGE THE WORLD; Reality is NOT FORGOTTEN IN OUR COLLECTIVE EXISTENCE. But unlike a drone that can climb into the Heavens and give us a "more encompassing view" we can only SEE what we "see" and, in times of darkness, it "feels" like blindness because it is Death.

I hope my country chooses Life. I hope my country stops vain utterances of "right to life" while ACTING in the MANNER OF DEATH AND DESTRUCTION—for they are choosing to, with empty words and deception, become but "creatures" vocalizing meaninglessness no differently than a lab rat with electrodes attached to its brain while it eats cheese in the pursuit of "knowledge."

In order to create a world of Life (a world where ALL life enjoys peace, love, generosity, and tolerance) we must first BECOME: peace…love…generosity…and tolerance. Amen.

Day 42:

You must decide whether or not I am a worthy observer. For if you deem that I am then the pages you read will be meaningful to you but if you feel I am not then it's best neither of us waste each other's Time (Reality's "gold" standard).

Below is a lengthy, winded, redundant and bombastic accounting of the most personally transformative experience in my life thus far.

I'm sharing it not because I "enjoy" being this "naked" but because I need you to know that I've seen things. I've done things. I could (SHOULD) be spending every second of the rest of my life ATONINING for my OWN sins, yet I can no longer stand by, silently—for my INACTION is an ACTIVE CONTRIBUTION to the "offering plate" being passed around in MY KING'S name…and it seems that the majority of MY FLOCK are unable to SEE that the "offering" being made in the name of Christ is being made to MAMMON!

So although I know, for the wellness of my own soul, that I should be spending my twilight years in contemplative repentance and ACTIVE CONTRITION…I feel I cannot REFUSE TO SERVE in this time of War.

Historically speaking, leaders (religious and otherwise) use their "line" or their "lineage" or their "inheritance" as a "pedigree" of "rights" no differently than a horse or dog or any "creature." Some claim the right based on David (Goliath), based on being God-favored Briton (Geoffrey and the Divine Right of Kings); all based on THE BELIEF that SOME were SUPERIOR to others and that SUPERIORITY meant DIVINE RIGHT TO RULE.

Okay. Fine.

If you "superiority complex" people (sadly, this includes the majority of my fellow Christians even if they're in denial or are delusional) NEED that system, then I suggest you REFRAME WHAT DEFINES SUPERIORITY!

Superiority MUST NOT be determined by the color of one's skin or the set of genitals between one's legs.

Superiority can NEVER be measured by one's FAITH for ALL FAITHS have tenets of peace, love, generosity, compassion, tolerance, and empathy—therefore it is INCUMBANT upon ALL THE FAITHFUL to BECOME SUPERIOR IN THE GOOD OF THEIR OWN FAITH…letting this be the ONLY INDULGENCE you allow YOURSELF…into this PHILOSOPHY.

Superiority Complex is a curse. It is evil. But, in my faith, FAITHFUL FOCUS can transform a curse into a blessing—but it is the FAITH of the Biblical SCALE OF MOVING MOUNTAINS; I am not that strong. I cannot hold that curse in my mind's way of "seeing" and exert the INTERNAL POWER it takes to "convert" it into applying it SOLELY to my own faithful FOCUS ON what is good, upright, beautiful, loving, slow to anger and quick to forgive, what is LOVE.

I had to completely reject it, as if discovering a cancerous tumor that I can spend the rest of my life excising but can never be "cured" of but, personally, "feel" that indulging in ANY activity that could "feed" it is too big a risk for me. Again, I'm not that strong.

Perhaps you are—tools are but tools—Stotan method works for me but probably not for many others: but the World is calling us all to come together, to share our "tools" and "methods" because there seems to be a Binary War coming: those who can only see the world in terms of all Life as equally entitled to life and those who see the world as composed of superiors and inferiors.

There is no middle way between these.

There is no Prophet in Slavery for those of the latter worldview and there is no Profit for those with the former as long as one worldview PROFITS DIRECTLY from the MACHINE OF **ALL** INEQUALITY!

Now you must decide whether it's worth your TIME and ENERGY to wade through the Muck of me.

~~~

The Timeline of my personal Injury, Reaction, and Evolution:

A few years ago I was diagnosed with heart failure. Having been an athlete my whole life I wasn't surprised to learn that I had an "athlete's" heart, in that my left ventricle was not only enlarged but had lost flexibility; my sport of choice has always been weightlifting—terrific pressure adaptively changed my muscles to what I wanted them to be but I've discovered that, in this life, there is always a "price" and the adaptive change in my body that I desired (bigger and stronger muscle) had "cost" me the same in my heart (which is a negative consequence).

Because of the "charity" of my State (a State that was forced to "legally compel" a percentage of people to "act charitably" towards someone "like" me) I was able to get a cardiac workup.

In addition to my "athlete's" heart (an outcome I expected because a significant percentage of athletes/laborers will have "enlarged" hearts as a result of chronic exposure to heavy burden) I learned that a "new" condition was my "new" reality: left bundle branch block (one of the three main nerves directing electrical impulses through my heart had failed—had "died"—resulting in my heart being forever-after…more or less…out of sync).

I say "new" because my doctors wanted me to accept their theory—that I'd probably ALWAYS had LBBB but I probably—like most people—simply hadn't "noticed" it before.

The problem with that "theory" was that when I'd participated in a U. of Alberta exercise physiology experiment on anaerobic threshold (with VO2 max) my cardiac strip was completely normal which established a timeline of my cardiac health and contradicted the theory of congenital defect. (Note: an anaerobic stress test is even MORE physically rigorous than the "cardiac" stress tests applied by cardiologists.)

What changed between my U of A "normal" heart and its eventual "failure"? Life!

~~~

So now I must reverse the timeline in order for the current moment to be properly expressed.

So first is last—the understanding I have derived from this experience is that, at the root of this physical journey, is the "balancing factor" of unintended consequence; the Yin Yang of my Abrahamic's Blessing| Curse.

     -If I wouldn't have been diagnosed with heart failure I never would have created The Living Project.

     -If I wouldn't have been poor I wouldn't have been able to afford getting diagnosed with heart failure. (Note: even when I worked as a deputy Sheriff I couldn't have afforded the copay.)

-I wouldn't have risked poverty if I'd been a better "gambler": I'd assumed that I—like all the other women I knew—would have the cake of being a fulltime homemaker, housewife, and stay-at-home mom while my kids were too young for school and then have the "opportunity" to eat THE CAKE (that I'd get to work and earn my own money) when they went off to school and, as a middleclass woman married to a medical professional, I assumed that "work" would be part-time so that I could be a full-time "mom" to the children when they weren't in school. BUT I AM NOT A GOOD GAMBLER (retrospectively, I thank God for that fact).

But enough about Me—for now—it's time for the "us" in this equation = I would not have become poor if my husband had not become fully disabled when I was 34 years old with two children under the age of 10 (and the "charity" of my State "legally compelled" my disabled husband and his family from a second marriage to "act charitably" towards his first wife and her two children).

16 years began with the doctors told us that my husband's complete disability was imminent (I was thankful for the professional courtesy the doctor extended to my husband by, candidly, suggesting something along the lines of "best get your things in order"). My husband always followed his doctor's orders. So we made serious adjustments to our "discretionable" spending. This was my first foray into zero-sum triage since getting married and being as I wanted nothing more than to be a "good" wife to a disabled husband and a "good" mother of small children—this meant that I went last, financially and otherwise, from that moment forward.

That was the "cost" of disease and disability halving our income—the devastating blow…the knockout punch…came when, without warning, the landlord my husband had subleased from absconded in the middle of the night—when my husband went to work one morning the front doors were chained and Bank officers informed us that the landlord had fled town—such abrupt and complete cessation of all income is, well, a special form of devastation.

That's when we really hit rock bottom. In 24 hours we'd lost all our income. So we did what most people do, if they can—we turned to our families.

My family was working poor. His family was well off. One of my husband's favorite quotes from a tour guide in Ireland commenting on a vacationer's fawning over the wide swaths of verdant beauty; the guide said, "Sure it's pretty. But you can't eat it."

It felt natural, then, to move our family to the Midwest. His family was well off.

I'd made clear that I wanted to live a self-sufficient farming life, for personal not commercial purpose, so that I could raise organic foods for my husband and children (as we had no ability to afford it otherwise and I knew eating healthy food, living a healthy life, was ESSENTIAL for CHILDREN and the DISABLED.

In response the Patriarch promised we'd always have a home and that he was 100% against himself being put into a nursing home or assisted living.

My mistake was in interpreting this to mean that the contract we'd entered into meant that, with his wealth, he (and his wife) would ensure we always were provided a home by them and that he valued the disabled being taken care of at home (as his own brother's wealth afforded him as he died from ALS) and my part of the contract was that I'd forego my own, personal financial security (a middleclass income-earning career) in order to BE THE ONE TO CARETAKE HIS SON—outside institutionalization—until DEATH.

I made this mistake because I wasn't able to see that the Patriarch's motivation wasn't for his son (or me or his grandchildren) but because he'd been diagnosed with Parkinson's only FIVE YEARS EARLIER and he wanted his son to "come home" and "be there" for HIM.

Needless to say, his half measures and empty promises introduced me to the character named, Politician.

8 years. Hyperbolically, as if Biblical, I served my husband and his family and taught my sons to serve them as well, honoring our shared "Abrahamic" faith but I began to see, bit by bit, the hypocrisy…the corruption…and the cruelty. 8 years an outsider of the Tent as if Pink in the "Bible" belt where I'd been, mistakenly, led to believe was a "better" culture for raising children. This began the simmering rage for the callousness of his Tribe when referring to ALL children (all people, all life) because it become unmistakably clear that his Tribe believed that some people were "inferior" and some were "superior", always "saying" that this superiority complex was only "spiritual" (in "those dirty rotten sinners and I'm a dirty rotten sinner" but when the single mother's getting food at the food bank ask for an extra can of mandarin oranges it's "those people who can get a 3lb bag of fresh oranges but go for the mandarin oranges because they're…" and the list of what words would be attached to that sentiment were exchangeable…in other words, I heard her say, "everyone's a dirty rotten sinner…but some like her and 'worse' than me because I'd feed my family the fresh oranges, because they're healthier."
See…superiority complex. This isn't MY faith, not how MY God commands me to be in attitude. My God wants me to ASK the woman why she's choosing mandarin oranges and ALLOWS HER ANSWER to BE THE ANSWER. Maybe there are more calories in a little can of mandarin oranges than in the edible portion of a 3lb bag of fresh and when a family is starving, especially children, EVERY CALORIE COUNTS? Who knows—I don't…because I didn't have the OPPORTUNITY TO ASK THE WOMAN—but the Matriarch did…and she chose to confirm her bias in order to "FEED" her own superiority complex than to do what her and MY GOD commands: love each other as Christ loves—to sit with the woman, to ask, to spend time, to give MORE THAN WHAT'S ASKED FOR. 8 years of what I would describe as Spiritual Hell, ironically smack dab in the middle of the Bible belt, but I say, "Blessings can be curses…and curses can be blessings—if the focus is Christ's heart" because it was after moving to the Patriarch's state that I got to have first-hand experience with what a "Christian" political agenda was…and, as far as I could see, it was anything BUT CHRISTIAN!

EIGHT YEARS I was told that my family wasn't "poor enough" for THAT state's Medicaid (though I certainly qualified in my home state). My husband got disability Medicare and a secondary insurance (during those 8 years his "donut hole" out-of-pocket medications were more than $600/month and most of the year was spent "in the hole" plus all the copays for all the doctor's plus all the travel expenses because of living Rural and having to travel to the City—one time I sat down, one of many, and figured out my family's monthly budget: unsurprisingly, my husband's expenses have amounted to, on average, a little more than half (not including the alimony of the first 3 years and the 21 years of child support). I'm no mathematician but half of a halved income leaves not very much left over for a woman and two boys (who, on average in 2020, cost 1 MILLION DOLLARS EACH from birth through college.

This is a very long way of saying, "In a zero-sum economy…I 'chose' to be LAST IN LINE." This meant that because we couldn't get Medicaid, I took my sons to the doctor as little as possible. For example, one winter my husband accompanied my youngest son to Devil's Hill to watch him sled. My son crashed, badly. I didn't see the crash. When I asked my husband he said he was probably alright, to keep an eye on him, and see how he felt in the morning. I was conflicted. My son was in such pain but my husband didn't seem worried and I knew HOW MUCH TAKING HIM TO THE DOCTOR WOULD COST—so I really wanted my son to just "be okay" not only for him…but because I didn't have the money to pay the hospital's xray or the doctor's cast. Next morning I asked my husband again and he said, "Let's take him then." So we did. It was broken. I have never forgiven myself for FAILING to stand UP FOR MY SON'S MEDICAL NEEDS (for 8 years my husband's needs came first and most…and I failed, as a mother, to put my SON'S needs first and most…even though he HARDLY EVER NEEDED anything!).

I'm not sharing this with you to create villains or saints but to, as honestly and vulnerably as I can, share with you what MY experience was…I leave other's to share, as vulnerably and honestly, their own stories.

This is the backdrop of my decline, in body and mind.

It is never as simple as a heart "attack." It's condition of attack with resultant heart "failure."

After eight years, and the death of the Patriarch, I was finally allowed to return to the Home State where I—and my children—were, though the same income as the Bible belt, "poor enough" to get the medical CARE we needed.

I found out about my heart. My youngest (from Devil's Hill) found out that he had a disorder that required surgery and lifetime of medication, and my oldest found out that he has a disorder requiring a lifetime of careful stress management. The three of us, thanks to the Charity of our State, are still alive.

~~~

Price vs. Cost

The PRICE I'D BEEN CHARGED for SIXTEEN YEARS OF LABOR as my husband's sole caregiver while honoring the Christian tradition of patriarchal/matriarchal family dynamic, COST ME (and my children) our BODIES & MINDS!

PRICE: 16 years of watching my husband, a Stanford graduate in Human Biology, a USC graduate in

Physical Therapy, and a small business owner/operator for years SUFFER from Parkinson's disease, multiple sclerosis, and dystonia.

COST: 16 years of HIS LOST INCOME (and the LOSS of POTENTIAL INCOME INCREASE).

PRICE: 16 years of HIS EXPENDITURE INCREASE (both in his increased health demands but also

increased costs).

COST: 16 years of WORRY!

PRICE: 16 years of being a WIFE AND MOTHER IN A ZERO-SUM HOME BUDGET meant

> SUBSUMING my "expenditures" for things like healthcare, education, self-improvement, dentistry.

COST OF 16 years of MY LOST INCOME to be a faithful caregiver to my husband? PRICELESS!

~~~

COST of MOVING: the timeline of events prior to getting diagnosed with heart failure.

So we make the Exodus West. My husband picked the town (a coastal town, a day's drive from where I grew up and from my family, which I love). It took almost 3 years to RECOVER—I finally lost the "weight" I'd gained…oppression weights heavy…freedom is light. I finally got a chance to "breathe" after the needed R&R (the cost of bombardment is shellshock).

I looked, with clearer vision, at our financial future and realized that I had, roughly, five years to find a way to support our family financially because—once again—my husband's "income" would be halved. Having lived through that experience before, I knew what needed done.

But the "job" I'd trained for (to "teach" creative writing at a community college) was about as viable as being a horse farrier (a job I'd also explored). The whole market had shifted to gig while I'd been "caretaking" and "homemaking." I realized that I was, wholly, unequipped and lacked the SKILLS needed for the transformed market and the "gig" economy for community college wasn't going to "cut it" in terms of a reliable monthly income capable of supporting two adults, one fully disabled, and two adult children with "special" needs (I've suspected were the direct result of maturing into adults from children chronically exposed to toxic levels of stress financially and spiritually).

Being back "home" allowed me to revaluate what of my abilities were actually marketable—and I went back to the only job I've ever loved: working with my husband in our physical therapy clinic, teaching people how to do the exercises they'd been prescribed, and all the duties included thereof.

I loved being a PT aide for my husband but its income potential was insufficient for supporting our family and the "gig" economy was making the position obsolete (PT Assistants now do what aides once did—less staff for better profit margin).

I decided the best course of action for our family was for me to become a PT Assistant. I felt confident that I could handle the coursework (and I already had 2 BS and 1 MA) but I had to concede that the years of poverty, caretaking, and personal self-neglect had taken a toll—I was finding it more difficult to recall the anatomy I once knew SO WELL.

Still, I've never been one to back away from a challenge. If I failed, well there was nothing new in that so I was determined to give it a try…because my FAMLY depended on my success (even if they didn't realize it then…or now).

I got a job with the State parks (believe it or not it was quite a competition and I probably "won" because I was, in fact, an old woman). Every penny I saved in an envelope marked, "For Kim's College."

I am still traumatized by some of the sight/smell memories—but I soldiered on…because there is nothing I wouldn't do for my Family. More nights than less I cried myself to sleep on a heating pad, swallowing 15 extra strength Tylenol for the pain in my spine, my joints…but I soldiered on—because the "ends" had to be justified by such "MEAN".

Two seasons—couldn't "break" me…I was ready to sign up for more (and they wanted me because I'm *that* kind of worker) because the envelope got a little thicker each payday…each payday got me "closer" to having "tuition" and then—even if it broke my BACK—I'd have a chance to PROVIDE FOR MY FAMILY…if, I could then manage, NOT TO FAIL IN MY BRAIN.

If you're not getting that, for me, this all felt very Herculean—then I'm not worth a piss as a storyteller (keep your comments to yourself—fragile ego here ☺ Just kidding)

But really, I was focused and willing to make sacrifices of myself—predominantly—but also of my family because they could have really used the money I earned with my head bowed while scrubbing dried and caked bloody shit squirts from the underbellies of toilet bowls and shower stalls. One was in college the other in high school—both athletic and active young men. $2k per month (my first season was 2 months, my second 3): PT Assistant school tuition: $18k.

Acknowledging I am no mathematician, even I could see that I was short—by about half—and that was just tuition (housing, transportation, paying a caregiver to take my place because I'd have to LIVE IN THE CITY): the energy I'd need to expend (physically, emotionally, and mentally) in order to be SUCCESSFUL at school and in practicals would be negatively impacted by attempting a daily commute at my age, my experience, and my condition.

So this meant there was ONE WINDOW OF OPPORTUNITY (one shot)—I primed the pump with my seasonal work in terms of tuition (and also priming the pump in terms of my husband "accepting" another caregiver in my absence) because I'd have to use not only what I'd earned but part of the family's monthly budget as well—the SHOT CLOCK, however, kept the fact that the "time" our "income" was set to be halved was marked. If I could save every penny and if I could get accepted and if I could have my sons be my husband's caregivers, while we stayed in our rental on the coast (it's always preferred for consistency of routine and environment with people experiencing disability), and if I could manage my brain well enough to actually pass not only my classes but my state license—I'd become a PT Assistant at, precisely, the SUNSET CLAUSE of my husband's change of income circumstance.

It was as precisely planned as D-Day.

And so, as plans often do of women who, like me, have honored the Christian tradition of patriarchal/matriarchal family dynamic—my husband "sabotaged." At least that is "my" side of the story and I'd be a disingenuous storyteller if I did not include "his":

HIS STORY

According to my husband, the stress of chronic poverty reached a tipping point when his wife (with her three degrees, including a Master's) took the job of a "seasonal" park ranger (actual duties: housekeeping 90%, landscaping 10%) because she, anticipating an eminent change of financial circumstance when he turned 65, felt she had to find a way to support the family.

It was too much for him, as a man, as a husband, and as a patriarch.

He took every penny from the folder marked, "For Kim's College" and "gave" it to the casino.

He wanted to "help." He thought that if he did that I wouldn't "have" to spend my days in toilets. He wanted to "save" or "rescue" me. He knew he was smart. He's always been confident in that (rightly so, as he's one of the smartest people I've ever known) but only an ARROGANT FOOL believes they're smart enough to "beat" the Casino—or a person with Parkinson's disease under dopamine agonists like Requip and Mirapex that have been litigated for having "caused" gambling addiction/mania in vulnerable patients like my husband.

MY STORY

So, addiction inducing drugs in addition to the emotional trigger of a man in our society (a society where men have ruled OVER EACH OTHER brutally and weakness often results in fatality even if only emotionally) I still had reached my limit.

I'd been through the shit with and for my husband. I'd suffered "exile" as a servant to my husband's family. I'd suffered poverty and, as a result, public humiliation (being taken to court and having student loan money seized), and have to live with the guilt that I even HESITATED in getting my children the care they NEEDED because of poverty.

Gambling Addiction—a bridge TOO FAR!

Again, as with the first time where everything crashed around our heads overnight, I turned to our families.

I asked his family for financial because finance was the tool they had that I needed. I explained why I wanted to go to PT Assistant school. I was told to get a job at Walmart or to "use" the degrees I had already. I explained that both the community college gig economy and working at Walmart, fulltime, COULD NOT COVER the WAGE of the 40-hour per week caregiver I'd NEED IN ORDER TO BE ABLE TO WORK MYSELF (even with me covering 16 of the 24 hour shift/7 days a week IN ADDITION to working fulltime for wages). The executor of the Patriarch's estate told me, "Then put him in a nursing home."

I turned to my family for help (knowing they have no financial help to give). They said that as long as they live and have their land I and my family can come live with them. This was of great comfort. I now save every penny (and those pennies are few and far between now especially) for a "tent" so that I can live in it, behind my parent's house, because the small bedroom I grew up in (in a 2bdrm house with 1 bathroom and 7 kids) will house my husband's hospital bed and the room's not "big" enough for the both of us—but at least I will have kept "MY" word: until DEATH (his or mine) he will NOT go into a nursing home! Even if that means I, Kim, live in abject poverty, I am housed in a tent, and I squat on the property of others, for all the days of my life.

PRICE I PAID FOR POVERTY:

Something had changed in my HEART between the time I'd participated in an anaerobic threshold study for U. of Alberta's exercise physiology lab but twenty five years later I was diagnosed not only with "athlete's heart" (the "normal" enlargement and resultant rigidity of the heart's left ventricle that is found in a significant percentage of hardworking, hard laboring, people) but I was also diagnosed with Left Bundle Branch Blocke (LBBB) or damage of the primary electrical system of my heart.

This was a definite change. The cardiologists tried to say the LBBB was probably "congenital" (they argued that I'd always had it but hadn't "noticed" it).

My U. of A anaerobic threshold experiment and the VO2 max test I participated in revealing a normal QRST wave pattern while under a VO2 max stress test (far more rigorous than the stress tests administered by cardiologists) disproved this theory for my development of LBBB.

So what changed between then and now? What had changed in twenty five years?

I heard the ANSWER to THE Call and the answer broke my heart.

For the call was my husband's DISEASE and my family's descent into POVERTY as a DIRECT result but the ANSWER—most heartbreakingly—came from the "Christians" in my life—for they TAUGHT ME REALITY: that CRUELTY, APATHY, and INDIFFERENCE had prevailed over PEACE, LOVE, TOLERANCE, and GENEROSITY.

So what broke my heart, exactly?

(IM)PULSE #1:

My first impulse (revealing my bias: sociology) was to assign the "cause" to our collective failure to ERADICATE the CHRONIC AND DEBILITATING EFFECT OF POVERTY.

My bias: I assigned the "root" of our PERSONAL poverty at disease and its resultant state of disability but I assigned the ACTUAL ROOT OF COLLECTIVE POVERTY was Society's failure to STOP the PHENOMENA of disease and disability RESULTING in POVERTY.

My problem solving, seen through this biased "lens"—led me to "believe" that regular people (the bottom 90%) have one NO CHOICE IN THE MATTER, that we're "power-less."

This biased view led me to the conclusion that the "OTHER" (the top 10%) has ALL responsibility— therefore ALL THE BLAME—because they FAILED TO HONOR THE OBLIGATIONS OF THE POWER THEY WERE ENTRUSTED WITH.

This biased way of "seeing" colored the way I "saw" ALL POWER dynamics even in my marriage because, as a woman, there can NO LONGER BY ANY DENIAL OF STRUCTURAL HATRED (misogyny and –isms like "race"-ism).

This bias led me to blame my husband's gambling away the money I'd earned with the sole desire of preventing descent into abject poverty on his PERSONAL FAILURE (or worse, when I was really emotionally hurting from this wound, believe his actions to have been a personally directed cruelty).

But that biased "sight" is never the ONLY way of seeing; there's a reason why there's a LOG in only ONE eye—so we can, though still obstructed by a MOTE, use our SECOND EYE to for a more CLEAR-EYED view.

Im(Pulse) #2:

Reality.

My husband's MRI scan visibly demonstrated an injured brain, specifically to the physical location cognitive mapping indicates is the primary "housing" of impulse control and empathy.

IMPULSE NUMBER THREE: cognitive dissonance:

-Reality (sociology) told me that chronic despair leads to irrational thought.

-Reality (psychology) told me that ideation (irrational) if left unaddressed leads to irrational action.

-Reality (faith) told me that even though I "knew" those truths (cognitively) that I wasn't able to "believe" him "capable" of inflicting such pain and suffering on me, as his wife, and on OUR CHILDREN.

IV.	Impulsivity yields to conscienceness

-The Reality of emotional pain and suffering had triggered my personal desperation.

-In THIS state I came to the Reality that some "conditions" OBSTRUCT MY ABILITY to "see/recognize love."

-Just because I cannot see or recognize love doesn't mean Love does or does not exist.

-In my conditioned pain, suffering, and despair I can "force" myself to "see" by using Stotan method applied to my own FREE WILL.

-I was able to "change" my VISION not by changing an externality.

V.	The "reward" for this disciplined exercise was the Wisdom of INTERNALIZATION: If pain and suffering can be STOPPED from the external then I have SURRENDERED THE POWER of my pain and suffering to THE EXTERNAL SOURCE. If the external has the ability to stop pain and suffering it is ONLY BECAUSE I HAVE CONSENTED TO BEING

A VICTIM OF THEIR POWER TO ALSO INFLICT PAIN AND SUFFERING (See: Munchausen by Proxy Syndrome).

VI.   I now know that it is I (the Self) that ALSO has the POWER either to inflict or resolve my OWN PAIN AND SUFFERING…INTERNALLY—and the "powers of the external" have no authority there, unless I "GIVE" it to them, willingly or unconsciously.

VII.   This wisdom FORTIFIED MY CONVICTION: I am good and sick of being a pinball in someone else's MACHINE!

So although, from the outside, what I'm suggesting might seem like CAPITULATION…it isn't. What I'm suggesting is A Way…one way of MANY ways…for those who have suffered…to STOP THE SUFFERING by TAKING AWAY THEIR POWER TO INFLICT OR REMOVE SUFFERING.

If you suffer, let it be YOUR suffering.

If you despair, let it be YOUR despair.

If you REJOICE, let it be YOUR REJOICING.

Do not let THEM take CREDIT…but that means REJECTING THE POISONED FRUIT of GIVING THEM THE POWER they DERIVE FROM BEING "accountable" (it's as if we're on the grade school "marble field" and they set up their "accountable" card for us to "shoot" our "steelies or marbles" in hopes of "winning" what we DEEPLY DESIRE…only they make all the rules and change them in mid-play so that unless there is a perfectly straight "hit" on their "card"…they cry "FOUL" and "take" our "marbles" (aka our internal power for change). That's the "price" of that ticket—if you can manage to outskill the rigged Midway vendor the "prize" is STILL TO THEIR PROFIT—because the VERY FACT that you DESIRE the playing card or PLUSH TOY means that YOU…you alone…have, internally, accepted the BELIEF that: 1) they actually have the ABILITY to reduce AND inflict pain and suffering and 2) that you have SURRENDERED YOUR PERSONAL POWER to them by "asking" or "demanding" them to CHANGE THE CIRCUMSTANCES THEY CREATE AND MAINTAIN.

My suggestion: Make them IRRELEVANT!

I.   Need nothing. They'll have nothing to take that matters to you.

II.   Want nothing BUT peace, love, tranquility, generosity, tolerance…INSIDE YOURSELF!

III.   Refuse to PARTICIPATE IN ANYTHING OR WITH ANYONE (including employers, family, and friends) who are NOT ACTIVELY DESIRING the same peace, love, tranquility, generosity, and tolerance IN THEMSELVES (you'll know by how much of their "personal" energy is focused on the energy of "others" (yes, I'm fully aware of my own hypocrisy at this moment but in this time of FALSITY I feel even I must risk being a Hypocrite for this is a Litmus Test, a tool, to ensure you KEEP GOOD COMPANY.

IV.   Good company, of "good" intentioned minds housed in bodies actively participating in the DISSEMINATION OF GOOD—that my brothers and sisters—IS POWER!!!!! That my brothers and sisters is the ONLY power they can NEVER TAKE!

~~~

Now I must address all my brothers and sisters who have been either DECEIVED or who now—upon reading these things—feels "CONVICTED" but do not know HOW to break free (no differently than a being addicted to fentanyl, domestic abuse, or abusive power).

How I Changed MY mind—and how changing my mind changed my EXPERIENCE of my unchanged circumstances:

My First Step: GIVE MYSELF PERMISSION to Change my Position:

When I felt my heart break (I, literally, "felt" the change from its "normal" or occasional "flutter" in reaction to high stress situations like public speaking to the "flutter" becoming my constant companion—aka Left Bundle Branch Block (LBBB)).

I have no doubt that my personal suffering (and that of my family) damaged my "athlete's heart" by destroying 1/3 of its electrical ability (ie the chemo-electrical "surge" of high levels of conditional stress atop an already "taxed" system of chronic stress literally "short-circuited" my heart's electrical system;

You see, he desperately wanted me to take three distinct classes of medication in order to manage (not cure) my heart failure and perhaps had learned that the best way to get patient compliance is to solidify a simple image to what can be—for many—rather difficult concepts…thus, the three-legged stool.

The cardiologist wanted me to understand that the greatest "stability" for my "weak" heart was that of Triune or Tripod but what he couldn't know (nor did I share) was that every time he said, "three-legged stool" my mind travelled back to my childhood farm, specifically to the barn where the three-legged milking stool sat beside the milk bucket.

Association. Perhaps one of the most powerful experiences in life, prevented my rational brain from "hearing" because my mind was too "busy" recalling…every detail…of what was one of the handful of beautiful memories growing up as a child in a world all-too filled with ugliness.

Literally, my ears "heard" but I only "listened" to my craving for what felt SO GOOD—those associations.

And that could have been the end of it. Me not getting all I could from my doctor's advice because I got caught up in nostalgia…except the thing that happened was that my DOCTOR'S ADVICE BECAME ASSOCIATED WITH MY CHILDHOOD NOSTALGIA and once the two were entwined, neither able to be extracted from the other, I came to a NEW UNDERSTANDING that a hybridization had occurred in my mind.

All this "tabling" (I have a tendency for longwinded set up) is that—but for the fact of 16 years of poverty and facing the reality that no matter what I'm willing to sacrifice, personally, I can't PREVENT my husband' inevitable "fate" of being institutionalized BECAUSE OF OUR POVERTY…did proffer, what I hope will be ONE BLESSING—from my cardiologist to YOU and your Tribe: "The Three-legged Stool."

Yin Yang. Blessings and Curses. King David's cornered sword and dead child. It was all part of the journey leading me here…leading me to create out of my own personal suffering from of immorality and failure something of value to you.

My mind had birthed a chimera in understanding that what had been, what now existed, and what would be was all but a THREE-LEGGED STOOL.

And like any birth (after a labor of pain and suffering) the joy of my Chimera's Birth became, again, associated with the stool, with my childhood, with my Crone-state, and with what will be—The Living Project (a stable utilitarian tool to be used by all who'd wish to).

The Living Project is Triune/Tripod as it is supported by THREE LEGS:

> -The Living Tome (Asylum),
> -The Living Mine (The Optimistic American: Indictment & Conviction),
> -The Living Song (The Optimistic American: Voir Dire).

~~~

Day 41:

Astronomy Forecast for Friday, 06.05.2020: "Fridays Strawberry Moon Will Come with a Twist for Part of the World," by Brian Lada, accuweather 06.04.2020

"In some of the world, this full moon will also be much dimmer than the recent series of supermoons, not because the moon is farther away from the Earth, but because the moon will pass through part of the Earth's Shadow to create a Lunar Eclipse…"

> (Note: Walter P. Gibson's character, The Shadow, whose catchphrase was, "Who knows what evil lurks in the hearts of men? The Shadow knows…")

> (Personal Note: I learned of *The Shadow* (the pulp fiction hero from the 1930s/'40s) while interviewing the 5-time Mr. Universe bodybuilding legend, Bill Pearl, in order to collect data for the collaborative project, "Beyond the Universe.")

… (above article continued)

"On Friday, the moon will pass through only part of the Earth's shadow, known as the penumbra, and will miss the DARKER INNER SHADOW known as the UMBRA. As a result only one area of the moon will go dark."

"This type of eclipse is subtle and can be easily missed by people that take only a quick glance up at the moon during the event."

~~~

Factoids:

> -Official 100% @ 3:12 PM EDT 06.05.2020

> -First full moon of meteorological summer (which began on June 1st; on the cusp of Pentecost)

-Source for the following internally cited quotes is, "The Old Farmer's Almanac":

1) North America—Strawberry Moon "This name originated with Algonquin tribes in Eastern North America who knew it as a signal to gather the ripening fruit of wild strawberries."

2) Europe—Mead Moon; Rose Moon; Honey Moon (the "Almanac" posits that this latter label, as this summer solstice moon falls in June and the month of June has a lot of "marriages" (noting that June is named after Juno, the Roman goddess of marriage) that the phrase "Honeymoon," as part of the marriage ceremony can be deduced from "Honey Moon." I'm just reporting. Not my logic. Don't shoot the messenger.

3) Southern Hemisphere—Long Night's Moon

4) Northern Hemisphere's Long Night's Moon COMES: December, 2020.

~~~

Day 40:

"There's a New Beast Out There—Enormously Powerful Anomaly Found in Tiny Galaxies," author unk. Source: thedailygalaxy.com; astronomy, science, space. 06.03.2020:

"The Cow and CSS161010 were very different in how fast they were able to speed up these outflows," said Northwestern astrophysicist Rafaella Margutti about a bright burst in a tiny galaxy 500 million light years away from Earth, a new astrological transient in the UNIVERSE, that launched 1-10% the MASS OF THE SUN at more than half the speed of light—evidence that this is a NEW CLASS OF TRANSIENT."

"CSS161010 is vastly faster, heavier, and brighter at radio wavelengths than its MYSTERIOUS predecessor, AT2018COW ("The Cow" above). But they do share ONE THING—the presence of a black hole or NEUTRON star INSIDE."

Factoids:

1) CSS**1610**10—number 1610…the final year of editing for King James's Holy Bible (fierce debates over what was to be admitted and OMITTED—both actions being terrifically POWERFUL TOOL in constructing any worldview; KJV was published in 1611).
2) AT2018COW—"the Cow"—year 2018—symbolism of Cow:
A. *Egyptian*: Hesat is an ANCIENT Egyptian goddess in the form of a cow. In PTOLEMAIC times (304-30BC) [See also: Didymus] she was closely linked with the goddess Isis—a major goddess in Ancient Egyptian religion whose worship spread throughout the GRECO-ROMAN world. "Her maternal aid was invoked in healing

spells to benefit ORDINARY PEOPLE. Her reputed magical power was GREATER THAN ALL OTHER GODS; she is a main character in the Osiris Myth. Isis was said to Protect the Kingdom from its enemies, was said to govern the skies and natural world, and was said to have the power OVER FATE ITSELF.

    B. *The Cow in Hinduism* The cow represents Divine and Natural beneficence; the cow is to be protected and venerated as a SYMBOL OF LIFE. The cow is associated with ADITI—the Mother of the Gods.

Winter Solstice 2019: a novel virus in the internal universe of us. Summer Solstice 2020: Novel transient in the collective universe. 2018: Cows and Myths. The Number of a Translation Bible and twinned, neutron stars (Black Holes)…I don't know what it all means but I know it means *something*.

~~~

Day 39:

Two Questions:

1) What would "consumption" withdrawal look like? Could an individual survive those DTs?
2) How long can any drug dealer survive decreased "demand"?

First STEPS TO GETTING SOBER:

1) Accept that Life is out of control
2) Accept that there is ONE DRUG far more addictive than ANY OTHER: power.
3) A drug dealer is a drug dealer is a drug dealer—all drug dealers are Capitalists (I pray not all Capitalists are "drug" dealers, their drug of choice being power, but THEIR ACTIONS will be the only way to tell who is and who is not)
4) The drug dealer will ONLY act in the best interest of their CLIENT (their DEPENDENT) if it is in THEIR INTEREST because like ALL ADDICTS—FEEDING AND NURTURING their OWN addiction takes primacy IN THEIR MIND over all other forms of love, honor, duty, empathy, generosity, honesty, and vulnerability: no one…NO ONE is CAPABLE of serving two masters (no matter how much the addict's power of rationalizing makes them feel they can).

Next step:

Realize that everything I "throw" out as a criticism of "others" is but a BOOMERANG of conviction right back at me: for I am as addicted to "power" as anyone else. I believe I have some answers, I believe I have some "correct" ways of seeing and being, but the fact that I "believe" this means that I am—an unreliable reference.

Please, my brothers and sisters, I beg you to reject most of everything I suggest—for I am but grasping in the dark of this Penumbral time—and I cannot bear the thought of misleading or misguiding anyone.

The only way I can continue is by TRUSTING YOU—to be critical of EVERYTHING I AM SAYING…EVER!

Scrutinize, dissect, obliterate, disprove—I truly want nothing more than to be WRONG! There could never be a greater celebrant than me if those in power, recognizing their "drug" abuse has destroyed our "Family," finally get SOBER (not just "abstain" or, in political movement language: appease) but become PENITENT for the generational HARM AND SUFFERING their addiction has caused.

And like all people who love an Addict—I am fearful that the addiction is too established, that the "body" has changed, evolutionarily, and that the threshold between survival/life is about to be crossed into Death and Destruction.

Everyone who's lost a loved one to addiction knows why I tremble before the Truth: once an addiction has been established SOBRIETY is, statistically, irrelevant. Even unto death. Even unto the destruction of all who have LOVED THEM UNTIL THE END.

To have the "blinders" removed from my "Horse-eyes" and "see" how badly addicted PEOPLE are to POWER (at ALL LEVELS including a "normal" woman walking her dog who used the power of her white skin—the "superior" in a superiority/inferiority system).

Boomerang: It's never about "them." It's always about "us" because "we"—as humans in a singular biosphere—are the PORTION of the "them" that is, by definition (whether we like this reality or not) the collective of "us."

So if you want "others" to get "clean" from "their" addiction to power—Physician, heal thyself! (and yes, there's that hypocrite boomerang that just smacked my consciousness as I typed that).

CHALLENGE:

I now accept this challenge—the challenge my subconscious is, obviously, urging me to accept—how can I get clean from my own addiction to power?

First I must know what "power" I'm addicted to. The first answer is never the deepest truth but the first, automaton response is, "Influence."

For expediency (and with the hope of not abusing your kindness in suffering a Boomer like me) I will commit to you that I will explore, more deeply and thoughtfully, my deepest addictions to power later, in private.

For now I will go with the "easy" quiz question and see if I can solve "me" with you.

So if I'm addicted to influence—I am an artist, intellectual and Christian so I think I'm pretty well "hooked" on the POWER OF INFLUENCE—I must first understand what I get out of influencing people, personally—for if there is one truth that seems to be presenting to me its that I am FAR MORE SELFISH than I ever dreamed I was.

Facing the discomfort of this truth allowed me to Know this truth—which allows me, now, to accept that this is a "lens" I must always understand is "coloring" not only the actual way I see but also the ability with which I, literally, perceive WHAT I see.

So, I'm selfish. I am addicted to the power of influence. Why?

Because I'm suffering…and I want it to stop.

Well that wasn't so hard after all. Sounds reasonable so far. Sounds like if that's my "addiction" that it is a "good" one…yep…you guessed it…that's rationalizing—the Trick of the Trade for ALL addicts.

Okay. So addiction is bad. Even if the "intent" is good.

But maybe it's not the addiction that's the problem but the fact that the "focus" on my addiction is selfish…so maybe if I can be EMPATHETIC, legit—like actually increase the sensitivity of my brain's mirror neurons so that when I see one person cry I can't HELP BUT CRY—then my "addiction" to stopping "my" suffering then BECOMES, in my mind, ALTRUISM.

And yep…again…rationalization—because the one thing every addict NEEDS…is to feed their addiction.

So no. Empathy as rationalization (even if subconscious) is still selfish—and is still addiction to power—and is still MY part of the COLLECTIVE death and destruction of UNTREATED ADDICTION.

Okay. Back to the drawing board. I'm addicted to the power of influence because I am suffering and I want my personal suffering to stop (and I know that "rebranding" my selfishness as altruism is UNTRUE—lies and deceit are also the Tricks of the Trade for ALL ADDICTS).

So see—I'm just as much an addict as EVERYONE ELSE—but I'm trying.

I guess that's it. That's all I have for you. Try. Try. Try | an elephant atop the back of an elephant atop the back of an elephant ad infinitum.

Day 38:

Question: What was the ratio between "owners" and "slaves" on the MOST profitable slave plantation prior to the Emancipation Proclamation?

Hypothesis: same ratio as Income Disparity in 2020 (1-10% "owners" compared to the 90-99% of the "slave" plantation's TOTAL HUMAN BEINGS) with the most PROFITABLE plantation, (the top ½ of 1%) I suspect, was the one with the 99% slave/1% owner ratio.

Now I research.

It would seem a Stephen Duncan (Mississippi), according to Wikipedia, "His plantations yielded returns of US$150,000 annually. As a result of these financial transactions, Duncan became the RICHEST cotton plant (sic) In the 1850s, Duncan owned more than 1,000 slaves, making him the largest resident slave holder in Mississippi. By 1860, Duncan's ownership of 858 slaves in Issaquena County made him second NATIONALLY to the estate of JOSHUA JOHN WARD of South Carolina, which controlled 1,130.

MATH

Duncan (1) had (4) boys and (2) girls with (2) wives; the lack of legal status of women at the time (property/wealth was patrilineal) this means that the male "owners" totaled (5).

The Eqn. 5/ (1000 slaves + 5 male owners or total population = 5/1005 = 0.004975 or, literally, 0.5% (the same as Today's Disparity of the top ½ of 1%).

~Sometimes hunches of ghosts discern Truth before stats~

> Factoid: "He moved from Natchez to New York City in 1863, where he had long had BUISINESS INTERESTS. Ultimately, Duncan was what many of the NORTHERN PLANTERS from this time ASPIRED TO BE, and was essential in PERPETUATING the connection between northern success and growth with southern networks of slavery."

~~~

Day 37:

Those in power want to keep power.

There is nothing more addictive than power (if power were a drug then the best comparison to understanding its addictiveness and destructiveness—its morbidity AND mortality—would be to compare the destructiveness of the coronavirus species of "seasonal flu" to that of the Bubonic Plague). In other words, power is more addictive by an order of magnitude of 5 than that of the most addictive drug in our time, Fentanyl—and addiction is addiction is addiction...everyone who's lost a family member or friend to addiction knows the pain and suffering for EVERYONE in the Addict's Sphere of Influence—for the powerful…who are addicted to power…their "Ring" is ever-widening (5 degrees of separation). We are witnessing what it's like to be DEPENDENT on ADDICTS…now we have to CHOOSE: Codependent No More or the Death and Destruction of UNTREATED ADDICTION (even for our poor leaders, who can't say no to the Monkey on THEIR BACKS; when I look at each and every person in power, now I see their backs for what they are: their INESCAPABLE PAST—their "backs" are "Whipped Peter's" back—for they are SERVING A CRUEL MASTER! Power.

They can avert their EYES from that GHOST THEY BEAR;

They can avert their eyes, avoiding looking at the Ghost's SCARS, attempting WILLFUL BLINDNESS; but

The Truth is the Truth is the Truth.

The North rose on the backs of ALL slaves as did the South. To be addicted to power is to choose the Master's whip over your brothers and sisters.

But as with all things behaviorally addictive (eating disorders, sex addiction, gambling, cutting) I am confident that, with great PERSONAL SACRIFICE and COMMITMENT, our leaders can become SOBER (not just abstaining) BY WORKING THE STEPS IT TAKES TO OVERCOME ADDICTION.

And with all things addictive, some will be able to partake or consume responsibly—but every recovering addict will tell you: for a recovering addict there is NO SUBSTITUTE FOR ACCOUNTABILITY AND HONESTY. That's why it's called, "Getting Clean."

~~~

Day 36:

Before I knew a name I'd never forget (George Floyd) I WANTED to know HIS NAME so I searched: "Black man killed…

The autofill BROKE MY HEART!

In ___

In ___

In ___

for PAGES!

None of THOSE killings were the ONE I was "looking" for…but ALL OF THEM made me SEE that this CANNOT CONTINUE! The Civil War began but did not end. The Zeitgeist of Slavery is very much alive—its OWN GHOST—but I promise you, if I have any Spirit in me at all, that IT WILL BE OVERCOME! Our REFUSAL is the ONLY POWER it is POWERLESS against. In our time, in 2020, and in America—no one can "make" you work…because that is, legally defined, as slavery. How much power can the powerful shoot up if they have no money to buy their "drug of choice"?

~~~

Day 35:

Wisdom of Sherlock Holmes and Watson

It is the shared life, the "hitch", the "marriage" these two individuals share—their "communion" –that CREATES AN ENVIRONMENT where BOTH become the BEST they can, individually, be.

There is no argument that Sherlock is the "genius" of the two but the WISDOM comes from understanding the dynamic of synergy.

Sherlock would be LESS of a genius without the STIMULATION (energy both positive and negative) that Watson OFFERS him.

More importantly, it is Sherlock's "Relationship" with Watson that allows Sherlock to assign "MEANING" to the rational limitation of Sherlock's own GENIUS.

This is the FRUIT: personal relationship yields not only clearer objective understanding by helping the purely rational to discover "meaning" but, because of mutual respect, fellowship, and the degree of challenge only the closest relationships can offer—there is JOY—and there is no intellectual tool more essential to innovation than JOY—and joy cannot exist in work that has NO MEANING TO THE WORKER; not even when the "workers" are the esteemed Sherlock Holmes & Dr. Watson.

~~~

Day 34:

I.

"The Sky This Week from May 29 to June 5" by Alison Klesman, astronomy.com 05.29.2020

"The Summer Triangle"

1) Vega in Lyra—brightest/highest in the sky
2) Deneb in Cygnus—lower/East
3) Altair in Aquila—low in the SouthEast

Sunday, May 31st, Pentecost: Neptune + Mars share early morning sky. Mars, ice giant (giants were the descendents of Cain who were drowned in the Great Flood). Neptune: "Tiny Pluto glows at magnitude 14.7—a challenge for telescope observers under less-than-ideal conditions, but within easy reach of imaging equipment." (Note: authority + access = POWER)

II.

If Freedom isn't FREE then NEITHER IS BROKEN TRUST or CORRUPTION.

III.

Cassandra (or Kassandra/Alexandra; Ancient Greek):

"Daughter of King Priam and Queen Hecuba of Troy. Her older brother was Hector, hero of the Greco-Trojan war."

"She was a priestess of Apollo in Greek Mythology cursed to utter true prophecies, but never to be believed."

There is debate as to WHY this was Cassandra's fate. Some say she promised Apollo "favors" (marriage? Sex?) but she changed her mind and refused. Some say she broke NO promise, that Apollo gave her the Divine Gift of Prophecy to "entice" her (seduce? Wed?) but when she did not "fall in love" (sex? Marriage?) he CURSED HER; some say he spit in her mouth. For me, the most unbelievable comes later (see history of religious/philosophical transitions of the time) saying that she fell asleep in Apollo's temple where snakes licked/whispered in her ears so that she could hear the future.

Apollo didn't seem to care that, as a priestess of Apollo, she'd taken a sacred VOW of CHASTITY to remain a virgin for LIFE.

And her reward for SPIRITUAL COMMITMENT was: "Her cursed gift from Apollo became an ENDLESS PAIN AND FRUSTRATION TO HER. She was seen as a liar and a madwoman by her FAMILY and by the Trojan PEOPLE."

At the fall of Troy, while sheltering in the Temple of Athena, Ajax the Lesser is said to have brutally raped then abducted her.

Today, we refer to the Cassandra Metaphor/Syndrome/Complex/Phenomenon/ Predicament/ Dilemma/Curse; The Cassandra Effect "occurs to one, when one's VALID WARNINGS or CONCERNS are disbelieved by others." source: wiki

~~~

Day 33:

Before beginning I meditate on the Note I wrote to my-Self in the Dark: "be not attached to the outcome for what IS (what is Truth and Right) are FACTS regardless of outcome."

Now I begin a Case for Legal Sexual Abstinence based on the legal precedence of Legal Marriage as defined, in a Christian nation and upheld by societies like the Federalist's, as "the Union" between what is socially defined as "an acceptable" union in Two Parts.

I.

The Conservative Christian argument, that a "legal" union is defined as "between a man and a woman" is PREMISED on the Christian Value of BIBLICAL UNION—which is SEX.

So their argument is that, Biblically, sex between the same sex is a crime against God therefore it can NEVER be condoned either by the Church or by the State as it would—in their belief—violate the Ultimate Law of God.

Legal Jeopardy: Conservative Law has defined "union" legally, based on limiting access to the rights of marriage but the Bible defines "union" and "knowledge" specifically as "Sex." So to define "union" as a Christian so narrowly as to apply only to the sacrament of Marriage while ignoring the SANCTITY of "carnal union" as legally defined in the Bible is not only Hypocrisy but Evil.

For all Christians, based on the Wisdom of God's law, recognize that the carnal knowledge between two people is a permanently bonding union regardless of legal marital status.

So why then is Virginity and ALL sexual activity (all sexual union) not LEGALLY protected?

What is the legal age of consent between two people under the age of 16-18? It has not been legally established because the only thing the Law of Man recognizes is the "property damage" of rape.

I say to Man's Law: where your treasure is therein lies YOUR heart—the fact that the "cleanliness of the vessel" is legally defined but there is no legal definition establishing the VALUE of EACH PERSON'S RIGHT TO CONSENT WITH EVERY SEXUAL ENCOUNTER, including the first, or LEGAL consequences when rights are violated, reflects the Heart of Man's Law.

II.

The Heart of Conservative Christian Ethics will prove equally problematic in trying to defend against a case for Legal Protection for Abstinence because Christian Conservatives have promoted "Abstinence Only" to teach Virgins the Moral Method of "Union" as defined only as marriage—which is, Biblically, only a PARTIAL ACKNOWLEGMENT OF GOD'S LAW (the "union" between man and woman, the carnal knowledge, the sex establishes the Moral Contract) and Conservative Christians have even gone so far as to—regarding Right to Life legal arguments—to state that the progeny of "sex" of "carnal knowledge" (God's legal union) are PROTECTED BY GOD'S LAW (See: conservative legislation that prevents abortion in cases of rape, including incest).

Legally, they are claiming that regardless of the legal status of the "union" the "product" of that union IS legally protected.

This means that on one hand, product of an illicit union (an affront to God's Law) is legally protected but that two people, of any age, who choose to enter into a LEGAL UNION by, legally proclaiming intention and action of "unionizing" by abstaining from ALL ILLICIT UNION (meaning unions not engaged in through the exercise of God's established FREE WILL) are not meant to be legally protected and that legal action is not WARRANTED when their Free Will is violated, in Biblical terms, robbing them of their God-Given RIGHT TO CONSENT (aka Free Will)?

My Lawyers: Make the case. Make the Argument. On neither leg—legal or ethical—can this hypocrisy stand. I am no lawyer but I trust God so I leave the Wrestling of Gabriel to you with Love in my heart for you and my prayers for your Wisdom as you seek the Truth; the Truth will set us ALL free. Make the "SUPREME" court DECLARE AND PROCLAIM its Heart's decision for EACH decision reveals the Master served.

My Strategic Suggestion:

All parents of virgins take your children—male and female—to their doctors and establish their "intact" virginity; in a land of rampant rape and violation the "curse" is one we now all bear…so as much as this may feel a violation of your child's innocence your child's innocence does not Trump the Reality that A CHILD IS CURRENTLY HAVING THEIR INNOCENCE VIOLATED.

The reason why you must have the SAME TYPE of conversation with ALL children is the SAME REASON black and brown parents have to have with their children about a cursed society that will murder them—a societal failure to PROTECT AND DEFEND THE INNOCENCE AND WILL OF ALL CHILDREN.

Why should "white" children be spared the Reality of experiencing what ALL brown and black children face?

Why is YOUR child's sexual innocence (you shielding them from the Reality of ALL CHILD sexual predation) more important than PROTECTING AND DEFENDING ALL children's innocence from predation in a Nation where rape and non-consent legal loopholes and "Puritan" sexual attitudes have become WEAPONS DISCHARGED AGAINST VICTIMIZED CHILDREN.

You do not PROTECT your children by denying Reality—you make them EASY PREY!

So have the conversation with your children—make the case—but respect THEIR WISHES! They have the Right to REFUSE! We ALL DO!!!!!!!!!!!

Legal Basis REQUIRED to establish a Timeline and provide a list of Material Character Witnesses

If your child, after you've made your argument, decides to consent and have their "intact" status established, medically then you will have established the beginning of their sexual Timeline.

Next, have a legal document drawn up stating that unless further notified, with legal documentation of a "Change in Circumstance" in consent that ANY SEXUAL ACTIVITY has occurred WITHOUT LEGAL CONSENT.

This same Primary Legal Document will have your child swear to, "Tell the truth, the whole truth, and nothing but the truth. So *help* me God."

Explain to your child that it is important that EVERY SEXUAL RELATIONSHIP be INCLUDED IN THEIR LEGAL RECORD including date, name of partner, and circumstance with at least three witnesses, outside direct family relation, to your child's WILLING participation in the "union" (the legal precedent for three witnesses outside family relations is established in employment and rental application law).

But this is NOT ENOUGH.

Your child, whenever he or she wants to have "union" must go to their attorney WITH THEIR INTENDED and BOTH MUST SIGN THEIR CONSENT, legally—date, time, circumstance, and three witnesses.

To protect your child's individual Rights, they must be—legally—allowed to amend their OWN LEGAL STATUS/RECORD without fearing retribution for their action/inaction from those who have Power and Control over their "livelihood" (there is legal precedent for protecting those who want to come forward but fear for their personal safety and security, fearing retribution, for following their "conscience.")

If you do this, this will be the "Me Too" of human sexuality. If our youth feel empowered and protected, legally, from retribution from a "hostile work" environment (aka home life) for participating in activities that are WITHIN THEIR LEGAL RIGHT, and they CAREFULLY DOCUMENT EVERY CONSENSUAL SEXUAL PARTNER—having every partner legally sign THEIR name, attesting to the fact that they engaged in consensual sex on a specific day/time/setting—then the world will finally see that there is SO MUCH MORE

CONSENSUAL SEX THAN RAPE…but it will ALSO REMOVE WHERE RAPISTS CAN HIDE (and that's the "shade" offered by people not telling the Truth, the WHOLE truth, and nothing BUT the Truth…about themselves.)

Why this matters, legally? If a young woman or man has 50 names on her/his Abstinence Contract but then reports being sexually abused (from the least to the most being rape) then their detailed record of ALL lovers will be the Character Witness list able to testify to the MORAL CHARACTER and willingness THEY experienced in THEIR sexual encounter with the person they'd once LOVED—and whose rape or victimization, I'm SURE, is JUST AS PAINFUL TO THEM…for everyone knows it is a special kind of pain to witness the victimization of a loved one.

Let the rapist then make the case that he/she is a "whore" who "asked for it" (the "it" being rape and victimization). Parents—help your CHILDREN create THEIR OWN MOUNTAIN of evidence to the contrary!

REFUSE TO GIVE CORRUPT PREDATORS QUARTER!

We, as a Nation, are "Children" of "Parents" practicing Munchausen by Proxy—they created the laws to protect "their" property (including our sexual bodies) then USE THOSE VERY LAWS to FURTHER ABUSE OUR OWN CHILDREN WHEN THE PREDATORS PREY UPON THEM!

OUR CHILDREN—our Nation—NEED ACTUAL and Tangible PROTECTION!

They have the right to choose with whom and when they have sex. We should NOT have to traumatize our children in order for them to ACTUALLY HAVE the right to choose with whom and when they have sex—just as black and brown parents should NOT have to traumatize their children in order for them to ACTUALLY HAVE THE RIGHT TO LIVE & BREATHE—but denying Reality doesn't make reality any less PREDATORY.

But we CAN make it so…unfortunately, it means—yet again…as always—it is the innocence of the CHILDREN that is sacrificed because of the FAILURES OF ADULTS TO STAND UP and actually PROTECT & DEFEND THEM FROM _all_ PREDATORS! If you're not willing that your child's innocence is sacrificed in this respectful manner so that ALL children may, one day, NEVER HAVE TO HAVE LEGAL CONTRACTS and NO parent is REQUIRED to shatter the innocence of any Childhood, then YOU…your SELFISHNESS and your COWARDICE…is the problem.

Wolves be wolves. That is nature. But wolves will only be able to pick off sheep as long as sheep, out of instinct (their "creature" nature) fail to stand and defend the Flock…even knowing that the "defenders" (being front line of defense) will be the ones first consumed.

That is nature. That is reality.

What is unforgiveable, in my eyes, is the sheep who—out of protection of their "own" lamb—either run away from the wolves or cower, hoping it won't be "theirs" that's taken, or worse of all…conspire (the "acceptable loss" sheep).

No.

A shepherd protects the flock from wolves at any personal cost—and we, each sheep, are ALL shepherds. So the question becomes: are you a Loyalist shepherd, devoted to the Flock, or are you a Wolf?

~~~

Day 32:

I can't make this shit up. I mean I "could" but even my prose never dared such purple as the truth of the story I'm going to tell you.

My husband's father died from complications of Parkinson's disease (and an un-mended broken hip—a very sad story for a different time). My husband had been diagnosed with early-onset Parkinson's disease and multiple sclerosis just FIVE YEARS AFTER HIS OWN DAD'S diagnosis.

When my husband's father died I asked my husband, "If his path is your path, if you only have five years to live, how to do want to live them?"

He said, "I want to move back to Oregon. I want to live in Lincoln City."

The truth, we'd driven through—didn't even stop—Lincoln City but ONCE (while on a camping trip with my family at the state park where I'd eventually become employed to clean toilets).

I didn't care. It was his "dying" wish. Charity of Christians (in the church "Family" gathering together to help us load the Uhaul as well as giving us the "donation" they'd collected on our behalf—I can honestly say it was one of the most beautiful experiences I had in Christian fellowship. My husband's Matriarch paid for the Uhaul and another family friend (a fellow Christian) gave us their personal money (for which I, unasked, "exchanged" the last watercolor I ever did with my painting mentor, Mary Murphy, because she died shortly afterward).

The total Charity covered, approximately, 30% of the "expenditure" required; the rest of the burden fell, primarily, on my shoulders.

When we settled here we were drawn to the Community Center (our sons were pool-rat Lifeguards…and my husband and I have always been focused on physical fitness). Just outside the City's building is a large bronze sculpture of Abraham Lincoln sitting astride a horse while reading a book—I shit you not. Ironically, the local lore goes that the artist couldn't even "give" the sculpture away and finally "settled" on "giving" it to Lincoln City when the City agreed to pay the shipping cost. I could be mistaken, but I believe it's the second largest bronze statue in Oregon (second to Portlandia…which, I believe, is the second largest bronze statue in the US…second to the Statue of Liberty…but I could have these factoids wrong and I am not willing to interrupt this Stream to "fact check" what is, in the scheme of this excerpt's wisdom, irrelevant—but I still suggest you do…for the Truth is worth it and I am not the only one capable of fact-checking…in other words…we BOTH must do work and I'm flagging this as possibly erroneous detail FOR YOU…it is my attempt to be "transparent" while also being LAZY and UNWILLING…see…I'm just as guilty—Boomerang right back at me.

Still, not going to do it…because the vision is more important than the detail.

So the fact that I live in a small coastal town in Oregon that houses an unwanted statue of Abraham Lincoln on horseback reading a book—that's the important fact…and it is a fact.

The fact that we moved to this town because I was, as a Christian wife and mother, respecting the authority of my husband's leadership role and as a humanist I was respecting my fellow human being's right to die in the manner of his choosing, and the fact that I am STILL here in this town after so many events that made me want to FLEE it (a sad story for another time) has always made me wonder, "Why?"

Today, in my country, there are those who are claiming "legitimacy" by invoking Lincoln—I say to those who are, "You words, Sir—Ma'am—are not just claims…they are contracts."

I now see my town's statue differently. It wasn't a "White Elephant." It was prescient. The Abraham Lincoln needed in 2020 is the man, astride a Charger, looking DOWN—lost in the pages of a BOOK—while the "beast of burden" carries him safely to wherever the PATH leads, SECURE IN THE KNOWLEDGE that the mule/donkey/beast of burden will SAFELY DELIVER him no differently than the Ass REFUSING TO MOVE ONE STEP FURTHER (even though the "master" on her back beat her) for she could "see" what the master could not: the Angel before them who, sword drawn, would have slain both her and her master if she'd taken ONE MORE STEP IN THE WRONG DIRECTION).

Now the VISION:

To all My LAW enforcement officers: Refuse to SERVE corruption. Any "devil's" bargain is too damning. If ANYTHING in your "Duties" conflicts with YOUR CONSCIENCE REFUSE TO CARRY OUT THOSE ORDERS.

To be legally protected you must follow protocol:

1) Refuse to follow orders that conflict with your moral sense of ethics and, immediately, file an official complaint.

2) Comply with all consequential investigations of you—tell the truth, the WHOLE truth, and nothing BUT the truth even if your past actions are actionable and you are afraid—I know you are BRAVE!

3) When Internal's review is complete you will be reprimanded. It is not fair that standing for Ethical behavior results in being personally punished but that is Reality—wishful thinking does no one any good when ACTION is required.

4) If asked or ordered to do UNETHICAL behavior again or—REFUSE (wash, rinse, repeat steps 1-3) but in ADDITION—if you discover ANY CORRUPTION of those around you, especially those with greater POWER than you, REFUSE TO ENGAGE IN ANY WORK! For to work for any degree of Corruption is to CORRUPT YOURSELF!

5) Prepare yourself to be FIRED but don't let them fire you—QUIT in PROTEST because this is the MOST PUNITIVE TO YOU PERSONALLY (and this kneecaps the argument that you're a "welfare queen wanting to suck on the government's tit of unemployment) but I envision a very SPECIFIC RITUAL for your quitting that involves the SURRENDERING OF YOUR ISSUED EQUIPMENT.

Now the QUITTING SCENE:

1) When your firing is imminent, (assuming you are licensed for open carry) bring your personal weapons in a lockbox only YOU have access to and a change of clothes. Don your uniform. Feel every moment. It will, most likely, be the last time you wear it. Prepare your mind. Carry your lockbox to the building where you work. Do not enter the building (you must never again cross the threshold of corruption). Call your fellow officers to be witnesses—demand that your commanding officer take possession of your issued equipment| you CANNOT allow your personally issued equipment to be taken by ANYONE BUT YOUR COMMANDING OFFICER (this is protection from legal liability). If your commanding officer refuses to come and accept your equipment then you MUST WAIT until they do (however long that takes even if it means weeks, months, years—I pray, should the desire to break the neck of ethical change decides such Draconian measure is appropriate, that the Citizens will come to your Assistance—and that you will know Love as you've never known before in return for your brave and dedicate service to and Ethical World.

2) Once you've called to your fellow officers to witness your surrender and quitting, while remaining outside with your weapon lockbox and change of clothes, remove your uniform down to your skivvies (every total institution requires some form of "degradation ceremony" as a method of conditioned reprogramming from the individual to the collective—so just as you put on your uniform to "become" you must remove your uniform to "become" as a Rite of Passage); fold your issued uniform carefully and respectfully—as you've been taught (you are showing honor for what remains honorable in your calling and you are showing honor to yourself for rejecting what has corrupted

Your honor); remain in your skivvies; kneel; bow your head; consider all you've done—personally—that has done HARM; and, in this attitude of The Penitent—wait for your commander.

3) When your commanding officer takes possession of your issued equipment, thank them for the opportunity to work for them, and say, "I hope to return to work as soon as this issue of corruption and unethical requests has been, objectively, rectified and I hope you will JOIN me in THIS endeavor."

4) Ask your fellow officers to remain and witness your re-dressing and personal armament for open carry.

5) As a Citizen—don your uniform. Feel every moment. Unlock your lockbox. Arm yourself. Clearly profess to your brothers and sisters in arms, "I DESIRE TO BE RE-ENSTATED. I desire nothing more than to be a peace officer. But I will NOT RETURN TO WORK until all those practicing corruption are fired and all unethical requests have been reviewed by a quorum of Ethic Watchdogs."

6) I pray the media/press will be YOUR ALLY! For bravery is more PRECIOUS than all the platinum and gold in all the Universe—and, I'm afraid, not only just as rare but MORE EXPENSIVE. So I hope that those fighting to overcome corruption REALIZE THIS TRUTH—and honor...no UPLIFT AND SUPPORT, unceasingly, those who will lay down the arms of the OPPRESSORS (even if they have, personally, oppressed if they will, unceasingly and FULL THROATEDLY repudiate their past actions while dissecting their motivations for doing them so as to educate the Public as to practices, methods, and culture as THEY ALONE HAVE PARTICIPATED IN—confession of sin is Protected under the Law—then those fighting corruption must TRUST their actions and words for none of us can read a person's "heart" but everyone with eyes and ears can see and hear a Public Confession.

A Special note to My MILITARY: I expect the same of you as I do domestic officers, knowing that you will have to LOSE SO MUCH MORE THAN YOUR JOB. This is why you are OUR soldiers (why the Aztecs gave you the honor of your fallen souls inhabiting hummingbirds and butterflies not hawks). You who are called to sacrifice so much—your FREEDOM—just to SERVE YOUR COUNTRY...you should not be imprisoned for refusing an unethical order or refusing to follow ANY command of a corrupt commander...but man's law is not God's Law—and you who will follow my order will be court-martialed—I give you back the wise words of Spidey (Gosh I miss you, Stan Lee): with great power comes great responsibility. I'm afraid, my Soldier, that it is time to stand for what is good, what is beautiful, what is upright, what is generous, what is peaceful, loving, tolerant, and empathetic. If you are being ORDERED to do otherwise, they can take your FREEDOM...but they can't MAKE YOU A SLAVE to corruption—not any more.

~~~

Day 31:

The Holy Spirit's Birth-Day! (05.03.2020) The actual Holy Spirit's Birthday is "debatable", Biblically:

-Luke s says aid it happened immediately after Christ's execution (but, Biblically, there is little supportive evidence to establish a pattern of "instant gratification" which Luke's assumption demonstrates.

-Acts I says that the Holy Spirit wasn't born for 40 days AFTER Easter (a pattern supported by Jesus' forty day fast in the desert as he was TEMPTED BY SATAN). Factoid: in 2020 this birthday falls on Eid-al-Fitr.

-Acts 2 says the Holy Spirit wasn't born for 50 days after Easter (a pattern supported by God's establishment of Jubilee).

If Acts 2 is the correct version then the birth of the Holy Spirit (being 50 days after Easter) meant that the Apostles accepted their MISSIONS from Christ WITHOUT being indwelled by the Holy Spirit (unable to receive His wisdom, comfort, or guidance).

Ascension 05.21.2020| Orthodox Ascension 05.28.2020

~~~

Day 30:

The Stotan Method applied to Typing Rainer Maria Rilke's, "The Panther," with 0 errors:

The Panther, by Rainer Maria Rilke

His vision, from the constantly passing bars,
Has grown so weary that it cannot hold
Anything else. It seems to him there
Are a thousand bars; and behind the bars, no world.

As he paces in cramped circles, over and over,
The movement of his powerful soft strides
Is like a ritual dance around a center
In which a mighty will stands paralyzed.

Only at times, the curtain of the pupils
Lifts, quietly—. An image enters in,
Rushes down through the tensed, arrested muscles,
Plunges into the heart and is gone.

——

The above keyboarding exercise took place one month after performing the Stotan typing experiment on an electric typewriter—it took me less than a minute with three errors. In order to achieve zero errors (the standard and expectation at the time I'd learned manual technique—35 years ago—took me FOUR HOURS to, flawlessly, replicate but it was through the determination to see a course of action completed correctly and, through Stotan discipline, that four hours of typing on a typewriter so poorly constructed that the weight of its own carriage meant typing on a moving target, enabled me to LEARN NEW UNDERSTANDING OF MY OWN LEARNING.

This is what I learned, page by page, by attempt and quoted from my contemporaneous notes:

1) My most careful but also most out-of-practice ATTEMPT; I sent the first copy to my mother for Mother's day with a personal note (one secretarial student to another—one office working woman to another thanking her for teaching me, as best she could, how to be a woman in our World)—5 errors.

2) WOW! This is SO bad but twice as fast. I wonder which way IS ACTUALLY/objectively more efficient—the slow but careful (less errors to correct) or the fast with 3x the errors. Question: will the rush/time saved from this approach actually COST more time in CORRECTION?—15 errors.

3) Careful but attention wandered—after the first error I could refocus because only one error is still great. But each additional error increased anxiety (unsure of self) and led to "fuck it" attitude—5 errors.

4) Went faster after the first thing I did was an error in the quotation mark of in the Title—like the "fuck it" I have to redo it anyhow so I might as well try out my speed for the remainder— 9 errors.

5) Wisdom from noting a mechanical error: (an extra space occurred when my finger's typing speed outpaced the machine's ability) It STILL COUNTS AS MY OWN ERROR because, in typing, the DOCUMENT IS PRIMACY. Because the document is flawed and MUST BE CORRECTED, no matter why it is flawed or who made the error, it was MY error and my job to, "do it again."—3 errors.

6) Finally getting more comfortable but still out of practice—too slow ☺. Goal: perfect! Use perfection for the oil painting I'll do this summer on disparity, bounced check, and Rome burning—3 errors.

7) Error number one on the 12th word triggered "Fuck it—go fast" reaction—7 errors.

8) I tried REALLY hard to be careful—even CHEATED by looking at what I was typing (my typing teacher would have FLUNKED me for this for one MUST type perfectly WITHOUT looking down). Gist I understood: women must be efficient and meticulous secretaries who are 100% accountable for what they "produce" or "replicate". I used to type 60-70 words per minute, error free—oh how ALL might fails.

9) Attempts 10-13 done consecutively without any rest in between attempts (tried the aerobic conditioning model v. anaerobic)—errors too many to count until the thirteenth—1 error.

10) Two more attempts using the same style—too many errors to count.

11) Stopped "reading" the words and started "spelling" them with my mind and fingers. Was not any slower than in the beginning (the out-of-practice attempt) but with LESS ERROR—2 errors.

12) The next four attempts using SPELLING v reading—1 error, each.

13) The next attempt using the SAME technique—3 errors.

14) The next attempt using the same technique but becoming distracted on the last sentence—1 error.

15) Try, try again—at the end of this one I typed, "I'd love to see men endure this level of inanity just to TYPE."

16) The next 7 attempts I decided to try a "masculine" approach—where my typing teacher (a woman) taught me to always finish the ENTIRE typing exercise (because practice makes perfect) I noticed—even then—that there were some who took the approach of "I'm not wasting my time" and those were the ones who, the moment an error occurred—knowing they'd have to redo it anyway—just quit that copy and started a "new" one. They rejected my teacher's value of practice making things. In my mind, my teacher being a woman who—in my estimation was modeling and expecting the BEST practices and attitudes—represented a worldview…and some of my fellow students (men and women) represented another but, in fairness, the "not worth my time or effort" were, predominantly, the male students. So I decided to "try on that hat." I determined to quit at my first error—even though it made me feel TERRIBLY GUILTY (saves work but COSTS BIG TIME in the MONETARY-based RESCOURCES of ink and paper). The following is how many words I achieved—per attempt—before "moving on": 11, 11, 66, 6, a single quotation mark in the wrong position, 49.

17) Tried looking at typing while "glancing" at the document. This lead me to, subconsciously, replace the word, "ritual," with the word my mind inserted, "VIRTUAL." This let me SEE MY OWN BIAS—and to see my own mind's insertion.

18) SEVEN MORE ATTEMPTS WERE MADE using a combination of all the strategies I'd attempted earlier (previous attempts using strategies in isolation in order to evaluate which strategy I could employ to accomplish the goal of an ERROR FREE COPY).

19) On the final, error-free copy—4 hours later—I wrote: "Copy of perfect copy. 4 hours later! And all those versions. Accomplished by spelling v. reading."

~~~

Day 29:

The "Totem Self" I used to be able to begin approaching the Universe:

My head: Maria Curie

My voice: Samson (My voice is my strength; I betrayed it in order to survive in this world)

My lungs: filled with the Breath of God

My heart: the Heart of Christ

My stomach/intestines/immune system/urinary systems: the Farming Woman

My liver/spleen: Joan of Arc

My appendix: QEII

My reproductive organs: Cory the Witch & Doula

My cunt: Madonna the Mystic

My bones & ligaments: Arthur Miller's, Boxer

My muscles & tendons: the Propagandist's, Rosie

My fat: Cindy Vortex (from Jimmy Neutron)

My skin: Elle my Elephant (Bariboo, WI Barnam & Bailey circus)

~~~

Day 28:

Matthew 5:

-the poor in SPIRIT inherit the Kingdom of Heaven

-the MEEK inherit the Earth.

Pondering Christ's crucifixion:

   I.   The political and religious leaders of the time, preferring their addiction to power over the Messiah, PRESERVED THE LIFE OF AN INSURRECTIONIST named JESUS Barrabus.
   II.   John 10:10 (x twin) "It is written, 'My house shall be a house of prayer,' but you have made it a den of **robbers**."
   III. The **Penitent Thief**" also known as the Good Thief, Grateful Thief, or the Thief on the Cross, is one of the two unnamed thieves in Luke's account of the crucifixion of Jesus. He is given the name of DISMAS (Gospel of Nicodemus); he is Sainted as Dismas but, linguistically, also referred to as Dysmas and Dimas.
   IV.   Jesus says to the PENTITENT THEIF: "Amen I say to you today you will be with me in Paradise."
   V.   Amen means: "it is so," "so be it," and in Hebrew, "certainty," "truth," and "verily."
   VI.   Paradise is debated—John Milton argued it had been Lost but Regained.

~~~

Day 27:

"We must, willingly, give up our addiction to efficiency."

~~~

Day 26:

To change the world one MUST change oneself first.

But until one can face one's OWN DEMON—the "demons" seen in others are BUT OUR OWN MIRROR (they are the reflection of what IS in us—the more violently we "react" the more that reaction REVEALS to us the Truth of our OWN IMAGE…if only we ALLOW OURSELVES TO SEE our own truth).

The understanding, "Let those without sin cast the first stone," isn't a call to apathy but a RALLY for RIGHTEOUS REFORM FROM THE INSIDE OUT.

There is no such thing as anything Top Down except God. Humans must Inside OUT.

For me—this means looking, honestly, at my own corruption. As intolerant as I am of the intolerance of others…that is the SAME INTOLERANCE I MUST BE APPLYING TO MYSELF, every moment of every day of all the days of my Life, until I BECOME MORE TOLERANT.

For if I, with all my heart and will, through a seemingly unwinnable war within myself, CAN BECOME MORE TOLERANT of my own corruption…then I can begin to be more LOVING to myself…but in a TOUGH LOVE kind of way…not the codependent enabling way. I can, lovingly, remind myself when I fail to win the battle that I gave my best effort—and that I can still WIN THE WAR. Battle by battle, while SUBSCRIBING TO THE PRACTICE OF TOLERANCE and being LOVING to myself when I fail (with failure, at best, being 70% of my best efforts) I can,

Step

    By

        Step

Draw closer to becoming…what God DEMANDS US TO ALREADY BE!

~~~

Day 25:

Gabriel's Horn is a geometric figure which has infinite surface area but FINITE VOLUME.

Vortex!

It is also called **Torricelli's Trumpet**; Evangelista Torricelli (1608-1647) Italian mathematician/physicist, student of Galileo, influence by Robert Boyle, invented the BAROMETER, made advances in optics and the method of INDIVISIBLES, from a VERY POOR FAMILY (son of a textile worker), sent away to Camaldolese Monk (his uncle) for basic education, (1624) went to Jesuit College to study math, philosophy, and science—but…"There is no actual evidence that Torricelli was enrolled at the university. It is almost certain that Torricelli was taught by Castelli in exchange he worked for him as his secretary from 1626-1632"—little is known of him at this time (6 year span); "Galileo referred to Torricelli, Magiotti, and Nardi affectionately as his 'triumvirate' in Rome."

The accompanying Image: Image: NASA-LaRC Fir0002.public domain original file (2.976x2420 pixels) file size 995KB MIME type image/jpeg description date 4May1990 *English: Wake Vortex Study at Wallops Island.* 'The air flow from the wing of this agricultural plane is made visible by a technique that uses colored smoke rising from the ground. The swirl at the wingtip traces the aircraft's WAKE VORTEX, which exerts POWERFUL INFLUENCE on the flow field behind the plane. Because of Wake Vortex, the Federal Aviation Administration (FAA) required aircraft to MAINTAIN SET DISTANCES behind each other when they land. A joint NASA-FAA program aimed at boosting airport capacity, however, is aimed at determining conditions under which planes may FLY CLOSER together. NASA researchers are studying wake vortex with a variety of tools, from supercomputers to wind tunnels, to actual flight tests in research aircraft. Their goal is to fully understand the phenomenon, then use that knowledge to create an automated system that could predict changing wake vortex conditions at airports. Pilots already know, for example, that they have to WORRY LESS about wake vortex in ROUGH WEATHER because windy conditions cause them to dissipate more rapidly.' 'This image or video was cataloged by Langley Research Center of the United States National Aeronautics and Space Administration (NASA) under Photo ID: EL-1996-00130 and Alternate ID L90-5919. This tag does not indicate the copyright status of the attached work. A normal copyright tag is still required. See Commons: Licensing.'"

Thought: Paradoxically safer to take off in "rough" conditions—within limits.

One version of Evangelista Torricelli Quote: "Noi viviam sommersi nel fondo d'un pelage d'ana: We live submersed at the bottom of an ocean of air."

Another version of the ABOVE Evangelista Torricelli Quote: "We live submersed at the bottom of an ocean of the element of air, which by unquestioned experiments is known to have weight."

The first quote: NASA-FAA

The second quote: NCBI.NLM.NIH "Torricelli and the ocean of air: the first measurement of barometric pressure."

You decide which "official" quote you prefer—but without going directly to Torricelli's original document your "choice" for his representation can never be wholly extricated from your own PREFERENCE (aka bias) and your preference may not (or may) be what the Author stated—this is the Scientific Method: observation, information, speculation, verification and acceptance of objective Reality whether it confirms or denies your own, Personal, speculation.

***

The Angel Gabriel's Horn's cry ANNOUNCES judgment day; we rise together, we fall together, so make no mistake—we are, together, victorious or defeated.

~~~

Day 24:

21.04.2020

Source: European Scientist, "No, Sars-CoV-2 does not contain HIV genetic code."

I. "A molecular clock analysis using spike and nucleocapsid genes dates the most common ancestor of ALL genotypes of THESE viruses to the 1950s."

II. "There is no way someone in a Wuhan laboratory in 2019 could have AFFECTED the RNA code of a virus of the mid-1950s."

Critical Thought: if two government agencies can't agree on how to directly quote the 16th century Italian scientist who invented the barometer (Evangelista Torricelli)—meaning they have 400 years of knowledge/reference material by which to ensure accuracy—how can any legitimate scientist dismiss ANY POTENTIAL OPPORTUNITY to EXPLORE ALL POSSIBLE AVENUES OF enquiry regarding a novelty?

Questions: can we be sure of the quality assurance (physically/laboratory ability, intellectual understanding, and individual/corporate ethicality) from research in the 1950s?

Perhaps.

But only when considering—weighing—whatever that "knowledge" is against the "Times":

For example:

1) Terre Haute Prison Experiment—from 1943-1944
2) Guatemala Syphilis Experiment—from 1946 to 1948
3) Tuskegee Syphilis Experiment—from 1932 to 1972

These were human experiments conducted by the United States Government to study sexually transmitted disease; whereas the Terra Haute Prison experiment appears to have gotten participant "consent" and was focused on "treatment" of STD, some of the primary researchers became involved in the Guatemalan Syphilis experiment where poor people of color were INFECTED WITH SYPHILIS WITHOUT INFORMED CONSENT—and this SAME PRACTICE was occurring, simultaneously, in Tuskegee…on poor black and brown Americans.

My personal conclusion: poor black and brown Americans weren't even given the RESPECT the United States showed Guatemalans—my fellow Americans were VICTIMIZED and FORCED to suffer unimaginable PAIN AND SORROW—including the FACT that many of those who were UNKNOWINGLY "infected" (poisoned by their own government) birthed CHILDREN WHO WERE BORN WITH CONGENITAL SYPHILIS!

Where is the Right to Life outrage for this HORRIBLE INFLICTION upon INNOCENT and UNBORN CHILDREN?

I suppose they weren't the "right" children in the eyes of the Prosperity Gospel Tribe because those unborn children were of the "poor" and, in Prosperity Gospel, "sins" of the "father/mother" are visited upon their children and, in Prosperity Gospel, poverty is ALWAYS PUNISHMENT FOR SIN because "wealth" MUST be "God's blessing" (a position that, conveniently, assuages any pang of guilt for global poverty and disparity).

My Point: The 1950s weren't halcyon—for most—and all "product" (including intellectual/scientific as well as sociological) of that time must be viewed through the "lens" of Truth if there is to be anything of VALUE gleaned from it.

~~~

Day 23:

    I.   "Jupiter and Saturn form a TRIANGLE with the Moon Monday night (06.08.2020; cusping Orthodox Pentecost on 07.06.2020). Here's HOW to see it," Brian Lada, accuweather.com

    II.   "Titan is drifting away…" Miriam Kramer (author of Space), axios-science. "(Titan is drifting away…)…faster than scientists ORIGINally thought." 100x faster.

    III.   The era of the Olympians has begun.

———

Wisdom of the Pebble in the Shoe

When travelling from one place to another and, should one pick/kick up a pebble into one's shoe it is ALWAYS preferable to stop, immediately, WITH THIS PERCEPTION OF A CHANGED CONDITION and DO what is REQUIRED to remove the pebble/irritant/object/ "thing" IMPROPERLY INSERTED.

It is VITAL that CORRECTIVE ACTION immediately follows PERCEPTION OF CHANGE because it is at that moment of new understanding that the VICTIM is MOST SENSITIZED to the Disruptor.

If one can't (though the proper verb, in many cases, is "won't") stop, immediately, and CORRECT THE PROBLEM POSED TO THEM in that exact moment, if they are determined to do it THEIR way (not respecting either the "object/disruptor/thing" or the PROCESS of CORRECTING) then ADAPTATION occurs in the form of DESENSITIZATION.

Desensitization—like all addiction—is not an unkind "tool." Desensitization enables us to anaesthetize us from our pain no differently than POWER or Fentanyl but—as with all anaesthetics—their RELIEF IS IMPERMANENT.

The "painful conditions" of Life are PERMANENT.

An impermanent remedy applied to a permanent condition RESULTS IN DESENSITIZATION (addiction to anything is the end stage of desensitization—a sign/symptom of impending Destruction unto Death).

The Traveler, upon noticing a stone in his shoe and REFUSING to stop and PERFORM THE PROPER/NECESSARY INTERVENTION, is causing SUFFERING:

-Suffering of their own Self by forcing the flesh to harden/callous by their refusal to remove the irritating Object; for the Biologic suffering is dynamic.

-Suffering for the Object by forcing it to remain where it—without the Traveler's interference—would not be being worn/ground down; for the Static the suffering is erosive.

-Suffering for the Vessel IN WHICH THESE TWO FORCES—a "will" v. a "destiny"—come into DIRECT CONFLICT; for the Vessel the suffering is Degradation unto Destruction.

——

Pondering Moses Freeing the Slaves:

The suffering of the "slave" is "exploited" by the "Masters" because it is Profitable and profit is a leg in the three-legged stool of Power.

But the Master's were never GIVEN THE GIFT of suffering—so they will BE HYPER-SENSITIZED to the suffering of LOSING POWER.

I see an Owner. He is walking along with the World BENEATH HIS FEET and his feet are adorned with the BEST MONEY CAN BUY.

Where the Slave walks barefoot—for Owners won't waste "good" money to "protect" an "inferior's" feet—his SOUL grows "calloused"...it CAN ENDURE walking on GRAVEL.

The Owner, with their protective shoes and believing their feet to be insulated from the world of Gravel, walks faster, with less caution, but no matter what SOLE ON THEIR SHOE—the NAIL pierces and their soles—without a Life of callous—will FEEL THAT PAIN…acutely; a biologic human body can PERISH if a pain stimulus is too intense; one pathway by which this can occur is the parasympathetic nervous system's neurocardiogenic syncope.

Moses "freed" the slaves—but when did the Masters FREE THEMSELVES from the SLAVERY OF ADDICTION TO SLAVERY? Addiction is Death—it kills indiscriminately. Slaves aren't addicted to slavery—so whose addiction is doing the Killing…which means THOSE WHO ARE ADDICTED AND KILLING US are the ones in NEED OF "REHABILITATION" and, in the Addiction Rehabilitation World: addiction THIS ENTRENCHED AND CONDITIONED require IN-RESIDENCE REHAB (meaning a "voluntary" admittance to a "secure" facility where "rights" are "surrendered" because the DESIRE FOR CHANGE (the desperation for change) has been determined—by the OFFENDER—to be MORE IMPORTANT to them, personally, than feeding the addiction that's killing them and all they Hold Dear.

~~~

Day 22:

Wisdom of the Braid

If you have not adequately (with enough care and attention to detail) prepared and carefully measured so that all THREE components/PARTS are EQUAL AT THE BEGINNING OF THE ENDEAVOR you can still braid BUT…for how LONG?

1) THE LENGTH OF YOUR BRAID DEPENDS ON HOW EQUAL YOUR PARTS ARE AT THE START; and
2) The LENGTH of the braid is ALWAYS LIMITED BY THE "least PORTIONED" part; after dividing your hair into three segments, whichever of the three is the "least" will determine the braid's "most" because as you braid inequality, the portliest segment has the ABILITY to braid the longest but the ANOREXIC segment simply can't LAST THAT LONG…so the braid itself (the collective endeavor) ends up being a braid that is not only CHAOTIC but also SHORTENEND—for when the "least" runs out the "most" must then be TIED OFF, leaving an unattractive and lopsided HYBRID of a braid/ponytail—and this is the WORST LOOK…for it reveals the LACK OF DISCIPLINE AND CARE on behalf of the Braider.

——

1) Last night, while in the tomb beside my dead King—consumed by sorrow and grieving—I birthed Death. 04.11.2020

2) My King's Deathday is MY Day of the Dead. 04.10.2020
3) Asylum Ranch, public "Trust" as long as possessed by a Manager, ALL are welcome, "Three Strikes" zero-tolerance policy for those who fail/refuse to tell the truth, the whole truth, and nothing but the truth—as there can be NO LIFE without Truth, only deception (which is Destruction unto Death), while exercising empathy, kindness, and generosity those who cannot be truthful—who do harm to others and to themselves—must be given three opportunities to make the CHANGE THEY WISH TO MAKE FOR THEMSELVES…but if they are too far into their addiction…the Asylum Ranch cannot be a place where active addicts abuse recovering addicts (and ALL are addicted to something). So, three strikes is the "best" option I can find to "balance" the desire to help addicts recover (a Herculean feat) but also "protect" addicts from the PATTERN OF ABUSE THAT IS AT THE ROOT OF ALL ADDICTION.
4) Paradox of Tolerance Solution: Death. If the Intolerant execute/socially engineer extinction of all the Tolerant then THEIR world will be populated by the Intolerant who, by Nature, will be INCAPABLE OF TOLERATING THE INTOLERANT—ergo, extinction. Intolerance leads to death. Period. The Tolerant, by nature, tolerate the intolerant—ergo survival of the species is DEPENDENT UPON THE TOLERANT SURVIVING.

———

04.05.2020

A Dream of Anarchy

1) A small group of 10-12 were at my house. With the world in Chaos and provision of basic/essential needs in jeopardy (unpredictable and unreliable);
2) The food IS running out. When asked, I say that we keep doing whatever we are doing in terms of our Individual Callings—even if that is to leisure or contemplation—until ALL the food is gone;
3) Then I suggest we ask our neighbor—who is a very disciplined planner (her Calling, which I am, admittedly, "less"-abled in) for Food/Sustenance.
4) One in the group says, "We should force her to give us what we NEED."
5) I reply, "There is no such thing as Giving…through FORCE…only Taking."
6) I bring my group to my Neighbor—a Woman with SMALL Children; my group is ALL ADULT males and females. Upon seeing 10-12 adults at her door in a time of Chaos, I interpret her expressions to be of Fear and Anxiety.
7) I ask her if she could "spare" anything at all for My People.
8) She "agrees," rushes off and returns quickly with "something" to "hand over."
9) I stop her and say, "It is obvious that you—like The Little Red Hen—have been better prepared than My People. I know YOU ALSO NEED what you are "offering" just as

Desperately. I am thankful for your willingness to "share" but as we—obviously—are not as well-prepared or disciplined as you…would you HELP US?

10) She seems genuinely confused. She seems even more frightened/anxious but also angry at being "asked" to do even MORE than sacrifice what she and HER CHILDREN NEED just as badly but—with a gang of 10-12 adults—has accepted Reality (that the gang can "take" what she doesn't "give"…and the "taking" is always worse—on the Children).

11) I say, "My People began to starve this day. We will go, forage, and beg but if we fail—UTTERLY—will you give me your word that the "AID" you've promised to give this moment WILL BE PUT ASIDE FOR US? In return, I give you my word that I will NOT return for it unless we, without it, face CERTAIN DEATH FROM DEPRIVATION."

12) What I interpret as her fear then seems to give way to Suspicion.

13) I continue, "And WE PROMISE to be understanding and PEACEFUL if you MUST USE what you "promised" if it is NEEDED TO KEEP YOUR CHILDREN ALIVE…and HEALTHY. In order for your children to remain alive and to keep health they need YOU to provide for THEIR NEEDS. So if YOU need the food…as Mother…please, PLEASE EAT…and know that we—My People—will be GRATEFUL FOR YOUR CARE OF YOUR CHILDREN."

14) I interpret her fear and suspicion giving way to Neutrality.

15) I said, "Also, I'd like to leave TWO of My People with you to HELP YOU in ANY WAY you need (gardening, laundry, childcare, housework, chores, ANYTHING THAT IS MORAL) so that the FOOD YOU'RE SACRIFICING FOR OUR NEEDS is not only a Burden upon you and your Family BUT A BLESSING."

16) I see Fear return to her expression; this is the PRICE OF BROKEN TRUST.

17) I say, "But if you don't WISH that, then it won't happen. They are NOT "guarding our supplies" (as in, we now know what you have and we intend on 'protecting' it for 'us', aka Self-ishness) but to be YOUR SERVANTS—as you have agreed to be OUR servant by giving us FOOD.

18) Suspicion returns to the Mother—this is the Reality OUR World.

BITTER FRUIT

Truth: our conditioned response to Shared Experience to what is good, upright, generous, altruistic, communal, empathetic, sympathetic, and LOVING having been CONDITIONED OR PREDICATED upon ACCEPTING what is evil, degenerate, miserly, selfish, self-focussed, individualistic, desensitized, and hateful has created a WORLD OF FEAR, SUSPICION, and ANXIETY.

-If you trust a Stranger then you (and all you love) are in every "danger" you can imagine (Remember that quote: "There is nothing in this world that can trouble you as much as your own thoughts," and the fact that we began teaching our children, "Stranger Danger," decades ago).

-This is a Lie: there ARE sociopaths but they are as RARE as a Human Chimera (yes they do exist)…but neither are the NORM! They are STATISTICALLY IRRELEVANT but we FEAR…as IF they ARE the Norm. Their miniscule reality of their objective prevalence (that of the sociopath and the Chimera) makes FEARING THEM IRRATIONAL.

-Nothing in the world is more profitable for Evil than IRRATIONAL fear for it gives cover to what we NEED to be, RATIONALLY, AFRAID OF.

~~~

Day 21:

I.

8.03 Physics III(Sp2003) Physics III: Vibrations and waves (undergrad) Instructor Prof Yen-Jie Lee (3rd section of yearlong series: 8.01 Physics I: Classical Mechanics, 8.02 Physics II: Electricity & Magnetism): sound wave (cm) water wave (cm) electromagnetic wave (em) BRAIN WAVE (em) probability density wave (qm) gravitational wave; WE CANNOT RECOGNIZE THE UNIVERSE WITHOUT WAVE AND VIBRATION (light and sound), "Mathematics is our most powerful tool," goal: translate the physical world into mathematics;" while explaining experiment and converting it, mathematically, "…even though I don't know my mathematics will work"; Newton's Law, Force Diagram analysis (normal force); Omega; solution.

II.

MIT Open University course, Neuroscience and Behavior, Lecture 15 "Development of CNS, Intro."

-Audiomark 18:15 "Matrix means 'Womb' or 'Mother';"

-Proliferation/Chordates/neural tube/cell tissue/mitosis/spinal cord/neural tube thickens;

-The VENTRICULAR layer is called the Matrix Layer (the Womb or Mother)/field: Embryology;

-Shepherd's Crook's Cell: AXON, cell migrates, connected to PIA, ("tectile" sp?) layer, lost connection to ventricle layer but later it was connected to ventricle proving MIGRATION, nuclear TRANSLATION is PROVEN, choroid plexus—specialized cells—it "gets out" via specialized cells in cerebellum, in and around the ARACHNOID.

III.

Arachnoid—spider.

Spider & Myth: Anansi is a Loki-like West African Trickster God in the Shape of a Spider. Anansi was originally considered by W. Africans as the CREATOR OF THE WORLD. Anansi was the God of ALL KNOWLEDGE OF STORIES. The Anansi tales are believed to have originated in the ASHANTI PEOPLE OF GHANA.

IV.

Wisdom − Knowledge = Peace

Wisdom + Knowledge = Transcension

Wisdom + Knowledge + Agape Love (a Chimeric synergy) = Enlightenment

enlightenment is Chaos in a chaotic Reality; Reality, when "TREATED" (no differently than a doctor's prescription) with wisdom, knowledge, and Agape will be able to "MANAGE" (not treat) Chaos, reducing it, no differently than hexavalent chromium transitions from its toxic form (Cr6) to its even MORE toxic form (Cr5) until it is, FINALLY REDUCED, to its SAFE (or non-poisonous) FORM of Cr3 or the trivalent chromium found in many vitamin tablets.

The FORM of a thing in Chemistry is the DIFFERENCE between a POISON and a thing NEEDED TO LIVE—the same is true of Chaos v. chaos.

~~~

Day 20:

The Wisdom of the Boomerang

What is thrown out to injure/kill and is unsuccessful comes back to the thrower.

In aboriginal hunting, a successful boomerang strike results in the weapon and victim resting where they lay.

We mistakenly believe that is how it works metaphysically; ignorance is not a defense.

~~~

Day 19:

The One thing of Truth I have to contribute is that the LOVE Christ commanded…

> (Note: the TWO COMMANDS of Christ: love God first *and* most (see God's first "law" of Free Will/Choice) and LOVE EACH OTHER as Christ loved YOU, personally (see Christ's crucifixion for the salvation of the Stranger.)

…, the love of something Greater *and* the Love of each Other is the ENIGMA MACHINE OF THIS WAR.

All philosophy, perspective, Law, religion, economics, politics, rationalism—ALL ways of approaching Truth MUST use LOVE as the Decoder or Lens through which the Truth of the Way Forward CAN be revealed.

This the ONE TRUTH I have to offer from My Tribe. The rest of what I say, what I suggest, what I ponder is but speculation. I hope it might be of value to someone somewhere but I know, with every cell in the universe of me, this ONE TRUTH—is the _**only**_ Truth I have to offer You, my brothers and sisters.

Hot Potato Tag: You're it! What's your potato?

~~~

Day 18:

04.02.2020 Institute for Health Metrics & Evaluation at U. of Washington estimates PEAK DEATH (not factoring for second wave) WILL occur on 04.16.2020.

Imperial College, London, computer model, released "weeks earlier" (approximately mid-March/03.11.2020) "If no action taken to slow the spread of the virus"; 2.2 million deaths.

04.16.2020 Astrology: zodiac sign Aries (3/21-4/19/20) ruled by Mars, cusp Aries|Taurus, governing element: FIRE (See: Revelations). People born on this day possess incredibly high amounts of INTUITION. You are a PIONEER. You have a HAND in most of the GOOD THINGS that are happening in YOUR FAMILY & SOCIETY (See: "many hands make light work"), people mistake your self-confidence for arrogance. You LOVE SEEKING KNOWLEDGE.

——

Story I learned from a bodybuilding legend: while in his prime an old bodybuilder said to him, "Where I am you will be." It imprinted in me because it reminded me of the old Sailor conveying his Wisdom to the young Bridegroom. It also imprinted because it reminded me of Martin Niemöller (German Lutheran pastor, 1892-1984):

> **"First** they came for the socialists, and I did not speak out…" Source: United States Holocaust Memorial Museum, Holocaust Encyclopedia

To my mind, all convey the same wisdom: treat others as YOU'D HAVE THEM TREAT YOU…because there is NO other, there is NO you…there is what we ALL ARE…collectively human living within a CLOSED BIOSPHERE…so that, literally, where I "am"…you "will be"…as our wagons are inextricably hitched.

~~~

Day 17:

I.

Two words/phrases came (spontaneously popped) into mind in the following order: 1) "Ataxis" and 2) "Maundy Monday."

So, obeying the wisdom of "Calling" I looked them up—but I looked up "Maundy" first, which wasn't a Monday but MAUNDY THURSDAY (or Holy Thursday), Latinade for "command" referring to Jesus' COMMANDMENT to the Disciples: "love one another as I have loved you." The "This is my body…this is my blood…commemorating the Last Supper of Christ with His disciples—with the refrain: "…REMEMBER ME!"

Maundy Thursday falls on 04.09.2020—the day before Passover (the Angel bringing Death to the nation unwilling to FREE SLAVES) begins 04.08.2020.

"Ataxis" is "Ataxia." Ataxia Telangiectasia (A-T) is an autosomal recessive disorder primarily characterized by cerebellar degeneration, telangiectasia, immunodeficiency, cancer susceptibility, and radiation sensitivity.

Ataxia Telangiectasia is a rare disease. It is also called: A-T, ataxia teangiectasia syndrome, ATM, Louis-Bar Syndrome, and telangiectasia cerebello-oculocutaneous.

Sars-Cov-2 (biologic chimeras are rare). Biologically, chimeras are organisms/tissues with AT LEAST two complete/distinct sets of DNA—most often from FUSION.

Human chimeras are rare: only 100 in ALL medical history.

II.

Further investigation into Human Chimera

"In genetics, a MOSAIC, or Mosaicism, involves the presence of TWO OR MORE POPULATIONS of cells with DIFFERENT genotypes in ONE INDIVIDUAL who has developed from a SINGLE fertilized egg." For example, one with Mosaic Trisomy 18, means SOME cells have THREE COPIES of chromosome 18 while other cells have TWO copies of chromosome 18. This variability ALONE will be TOO MUCH for the current computational models to render. Somatic Mosaicism (vs. germ line cells) can occur during fetal development, genetically inheritable, TRIGGERING EVEN CAN OCCURE LATER IN LIFE (see: herpetic, MS, and the 1917 viral encephalopathic lethargica or "sleeping sickness" with advanced parkinsonian presentation). Asymptomatic presentation occurs ONLY in germ line cell population, so it can be passed onto offspring unknowingly. Symptomatic cell population phenotypic effect will depend on the EXTENT of the MOSAIC CELL POPULATION but no risk of passing Mosaic genotype to offspring. An example of Mosaicism is Mosaic Down Syndrome (95% of Down's Syndrome patients have Trisomy 21—an extra #21 chromosome in

EVERY CELL of their BODY. Mosaicism is described as a PERCENTAGE—"normal" human chromosomes: 46 (23 from Mother, 23 from Father) + cell division/mitosis = "normal" human.

Wisdom of Biological Mosaicism:

Too much concentration of "wealth" in ONE area of an ENTIRE CODING SYTEM NEGATIVELY IMPACTS the collective BODY's physical, social, and spiritual Reality.

III.

Recurring Vision: Stained glass & Mosaic

Years ago I wrote an Apologetic explanation for the Triune Christian God. The explanation that an egg (three distinct "parts" of one egg) was a good physical explanation of God as Father/Creator, Son as God/Son, and Holy Spirit as God/Son's Ghost just didn't work for me because the three "distinct" component's referred to in an egg are also chemically distinct—but in the Metaphysical (God, is God, is God so the "chemistry" is indistinct). To my understanding then, the closest model was Mitosis and the differentiation of Sister Cells—same chemistry different function/ "job." This was still not satisfying Metaphysically because although the initial "chemistry" is the same…the "function" alters the "chemistry" (in other words, the cells "evolve") so this would mean that although Christ was ONCE the same as God…because his FUNCTION was DIFFERENT than God's he TRANFORMED TO FIT HIS FUNCTION, therefore could no longer be "exactly" God (as the Sister Cell is before differentiation).

So, I searched on.

Until V-Sauce's "The Banach-Tarski Paradox."

The PRIMARY ERROR of the egg and mitosis as metaphysical explanation for the Triune God…was the factor of Infinity.

Banach-Tarski, by factoring Infinity, creates THREE EXACT BUT DISTINCTLY SEPARATE entities.

I believe that in order to understand Covid-19 we are currently failing to Factor Chaos (Infinity).

IV.

Intelligence + Wisdom = Peace

——

Einstein's Grief: Reading letters from the last leg of his life revealed the deep guilt and suffering he'd endured for knowing how his innovation—his Mind—made the suffering resulting from Manhattan Project possible.

Guilt and shame are the Mind's "Wasting Diseases." They eat the "flesh" away as if worms; try to imagine what could have been achieved for the betterment of ALL MANKIND if Einstein's mind had remained "unadulterated" (if his mind that had never subjected to the Abuse of Corruption and resultant guilt and shame that eats the brain like worms in the grave)?

Imagine what he could have ACCOMPLISHED if the parts of his brain most affected by guilt/shame/motivation (the Limbic System—which is also attacked by Covid-19) had remained UNADULTERATED.

In a 1979 Phil Donahue interview with Milton Friedman (Chicago School Economist; Trickle Down Economics) Friedman claimed that Einstein's GREATEST contribution was the Manhattan Project, saying, "It wouldn't have been possible under the regulatory standards of our time."

Wisdom says that EINSTEIN'S GREATEST CONTRIBUTION was his MIND'S POTENTIAL to SOLVE THE PROBLEMS OF HUMANITY (to win the Battle…not just war afield war ad infinitum).

~~~

Day 17:

Someone's great idea (not mine): "You don't feel speed, only acceleration."

[I'd tend towards specification so I'd state it as: "You don't perceive constant speed only its disruption either by acceleration or deceleration."]

Wisdom: we are BESTLY GREATEST when we work TOGETHER, Respectfully, with acknowledgement of each other's Right to "add" or "subtract" because ALL MATH is an ATTEMPT TO SOLVE PROBLEMS.

~~~

Day 16:

My Journey as a Christian:

With great effort and a focus on learning Truth from my Christian understanding it took 4 months from me to shift my focus from ME (my pain, my fear, my burdens) to US (my most loved ones including my Faith)…it took me FOUR HOURS TO SHIFT THAT FOCUS TO WE (ALL Life).

When I say, Focus, the specific focus was of the Norse ilk—a good death. At first I prayed for my own good death (painless, fearless, and quick). It took four months of facing my own death with the confidence that it wouldn't be "bad" before I could even BECOME BRAVE ENOUGH to give that up for ANYONE, including my own family. It took me FOUR MONTHS of excruciating terror to embrace, in my mind, the worst possible death for myself (yes I have an active imagination). It was only after I could face my bad death that I as actually ABLE TO SOBERLY CHOOSE OTHERS OVER MYSELF (fear is no different than any other intoxicant) but even then I COULDN'T do that for anyone that I didn't, personally, "love," but something about THIS JOURNEY allowed me to spend VERY LITTLE TIME on this Platform...for within FOUR HOURS...I, gladly, traded my very best death (no pain, no fear, instantaneous) for the worst possible death (suffering torture without relief unto death) FOR EVERY LIVING BEING if it meant THEY got to have GOOD DEATHS.

It was an exercise in accelerating deceleration speeding the convergence inside me to the place of Being.

~~~

Day 15:

Upon pondering Buddhist Death (contemplating self-evisceration unto death) using my Christian-conditioned mind:

03.29.2020 The first vision came on Thanksgiving (November, 2019) after I used my mind, body, and spirit to expel the Holy Spirit from me—with the last ditch hope that it would "open" the Hearts of all my fellow brothers and sisters in Christ around the world to perform a Global Heart Transplant for Christians. This was the most brutal experience I'd had to this point for there was nothing I loved MORE or BELIEVED IN THE POWER OF more than that of the Holy Spirit. To OFFER up as sacrifice MY OWN ABILITY TO RELATE TO GOD, to COMMUNE WITH GOD, to be left, wholly, alone to face Reality no differently than my Atheist brothers and sisters—it was the worst SEPERATION I've ever experienced—that's HOW WORTHY THE CAUSE HAD BECOME TO ME, personally.

It was only AFTER I'd SACRIFICED WHAT I LOVED MOST out of LOVING OTHERS MORE THAN MYSELF...that the first vision came but before EITHER (the sacrifice and the vision) came my Negotiation of Death with God so that is where I must begin here, in the before:

1) Prior to releasing my Holy Spirit, I negotiated my Contract with God. I asked for a quick, painless, fear-free Death WHILE accepting that the Life left in me would be determined, by the King of THIS world, as is "right" and Legal—for Satan and the CORRUPTION OF HIS WAYS ARE THE LAWS AND MORES OF THIS KINGDOM (Render unto Caesar) and I accepted the terms—that I'd suffer torture up unto the moment of my good death. I was afraid of suffering—even though I, rationally, understood that I had only realized a FRACTION of my personal potential for suffering...and that my personal suffering, relative to ALL my brothers and sisters, was—STATISTICALLY IRRELEVANT. But this "good death" Bargain with God was

not a Rash Decision. The Negotiation took place over THREE SEPARATE WALKS WITH GOD (in His Presence).

2) Three Walks: Three separate walks because, unlike Satan/Corruption, God does not want to trick or trap us into a Binding Contract. God wants us to CHOOSE, with our INFORMED CONSENT and THROUGH OUR OWN INTENTION, to do what is: good, upright, honorable, honest, trustworthy, healing, gentle, kind, loving, peaceful, generous, and tolerant. And, unlike Satan/Corruption, God LET'S US CHANGE OUR CONTRACTS because His GOAL is NOT TO PUNISH or deceive/trick but for us to LEARN (knowing that WE ALL learn best from our mistakes and failures because each time we attempt something we fail—or succeed—at...we are EXERCISING OUR FREE WILL (the First Law, the PRIMACY of God's Law as established in Genesis). Three walks to establish a Covenant with God: my "good" death in exchange for whatever He called me to do. This Bargain held for FOUR MONTHS.

3) A New Covenant: four months later—another vision. Terror. Horror! Sacred Heart Christians being hunted/killed/tortured—even my own family for even if my Family are not Heart of Christ Christians...the king of our World knows that the BEST way to torture is to TORTURE WHAT ONE LOVES MOST. (The Wisdom: in our deepest self we Know—loving others IS what We love MOST...even though our Actions don't Match our Hearts...not yet...but we can CHANGE THIS CONTRACT.) But back to the vision: When I'd negotiated my Contract with God I hadn't realized that the suffering I was "willing to accept" wouldn't apply to ME ALONE...the vision made me see the ERROR of IMPRECISION—for I watched my fellow Sacred Heart of Christ Christians being PERSECUTED...and I had a VISCERAL REACTION—I become Terrified. I tried to "control" the vision. I tried to "negotiate"—it had worked before and I felt confident in God's desire to negotiate with me even though the years 2027/2030 had pressed on me a sensation that the Time for negotiation was Ending. Seeing the unavoidable and universal suffering I begged God to give my sons and husbands (plural, third marriage) "my" negotiated death—in exchange I'd take THEIR DOSES of suffering/torture. THIS BARGAIN LASTED ONLY FOUR HOURS.

4) The NewNew Covenant: Four hours of meditating. Four hours I wrestled, as if Gabriel himself, before I could go back to God to Renegotiate. God, an ever-Benevolent Father, ready and waiting to faithfully renegotiate with me—his Beloved Daughter, Mother of His Children, and Partner (Bride/Help-Mate). I asked that ALL could have "good" deaths but I qualified that by "good" death my greatest DESIRE was that—when a person's death has become inevitable—that they ALL simply fall into sleep and Dream with Him without ever becoming conscious of the suffering Throe of Death—and, in this place of Serenity—THEN have a quick, painless, and fearless physical death ("To sleep, perchance to dream") but only if the person WANTS this death—for those who choose to suffer, fully conscience, I want them to fulfill THEIR OWN WILL. I was offering. As with any Gift, the receiver is free to accept or decline. My part of the Covenant meant

that I, as One Person, had to accept—in my mind—the SAME treatment as my King…and my mind is IMAGINATIVE! I was overwhelmed by fear. Not that I wouldn't be able to endure torture (for all endure torture and all fail to endure torture and I knew I was no exception) but I was afraid I would be too weak to stand—as a woman. We women are Life. We are the Bearers and Bringers of Life. It is our STRONGEST ATTACHMENT in this world. And I'm no Jesus. I'm not even a Man. I was not Designed to "lead"…but because of the utter and abject failure of Man to gird his LOINS from Corruption…desperate times have called for desperate measure—the Help-Mate must now Help the Mate…by allowing them a "time out" to reflect, to become penitent, and to realize that God is calling THEM to REJECT CORRUPTION. For God, in my vision walks with Him, desires that NONE should Perish.

5) Four months of meditating on God and Christ to transition from "I/Me" to "My Family." Four hours to transition from "My" to "Our Family/We/Us." As a white, female, educated, middleclass (status transitioned to poverty because of nuclear family disability/disease)…it took FOUR MONTHS AND FOUR HOURS OF PERSONAL SUFFERING…and, in my mind—in my Heart of Christ—this is so VERY LITTLE asked of me. This fact, alone, reveals the UTTER SELFISHNESS OF MY OWN HEART—itself, Corruption—these times call for me to "remove" the Mote as well as the Log—for now we MUST USE BOTH EYES TO SEE THE TRUTH that corruption ANYWHERE is corruption EVERYWHERE.

Wisdom: at the beginning, facing a torturous death was unbearable as I did not believe, in my own strength, I could endure it but I didn't quit trying. It took four months. It was as if a "war" movie was me. But by battling and overcoming ("killing") the "enemy" (the self) I was able to, honestly (not wishfully thinking) allow myself to be sacrificed for my loved ones (a feat many claim but few can…it goes against our "creature" nature to actually sacrifice the 'self' for anything or anyone). Four months of practice meant that the next step, sacrificing self for the collective ALL, only took four hours—that's the Ratio. Improvements in the mind's consciousness ARE SYNERGYSTIC.

~~~

Day 14:

A) You can Reach further with an openly extended hand than a fist: this is the Wisdom of Self-Interested Forgiveness (it is also the Wisdom of the Warrior—for if an arm is fully extended, the only "defense" is the "flick of the wrist open slap" compared to the closed fist which is, biomechanically speaking, immobile).

B) The Least will be First—in the History of the World (specifically, the histories of the world) there has not been ONE GROUP of Humans MORE OPPRESSED than women…and NO group of women has been MORE OPPRESSED and DISENFRANCHISED than Women of Color and no American woman of color has been

AS OPPRESSED AND DISENFRANCHISED AS A WOMAN OF NATIVE AMERICAN TRIBE: 2020 America needs to elect A NATIVE AMERICAN WOMAN FOR PRESIDENT, A BLACK WOMAN AS VP, and a WOMAN of any color to be SENATE MAJORITY LEADER—the THREE (the Trinity) need to run on the Platform of **REFORM**. This Year of the Woman isn't about Sexism…it's about the Bringers of Life (the Repairers of the Breach) saving us from Death. Whichever women accept this Herculean Burden—their "umbra" MUST be "REFORM" (racism, sexism, anti-humanitarianism are just different "outfits" donned by the same Corporeal Body: Corruption).

C) THE YEAR OF THE TRIUNE CHIMERA: In this War imagine the coalition of WWII: American White women and the White men who love them+American Black women and men+Native & Mexican American women and men=Allied Force. Defeating Corruption will take EVERYTHING/FULL EFFORT from the Triune (David's Goliath was the Victory of Individualism; 2020's Goliath will be the Victory of Collectivism) but the outcome of this War (as with WWII) is NOT ASSURED. ican land will be destroyed as if London and Whites will make use "their" funding and lives (yes it is NOT "theirs" it is ILL-GOTTEN GAIN FROM A CORRUPT SYSTEM…but the time to address this issue is after—God willing—the War is won).

D) May we PLEASE not forget the lessons of WWII Peace! Dear God, please make us REMEMBER: Grievance is the ROOT of CORRUPTION! Corruption can't grow without it. If we "kill" corruption at its root—if we RESOLVE GRIEVANCE—then we will be able to "easily"—through Vigilance—keep our "Garden" free of the Weeds that are STARVING the World of Nutrient. Winning "this" War will take everything we've got…and winning this war is the EASIEST THING IN THE WORLD compared to ESTABLISHNG LASTING PEACE. Let us, with the head of a black woman, the heart of Native American People, the Strength of Black and Brown People, and the ill-gotten gains of White People actually REALIZE the Arthurian "myth" of a Round/Circle (The Feminine is portrayed as rounded because it is the Bringer of Life—even Arthurian Legend acknowledges the power of the Woman in establishing Peace Negotiation). It is time for the CORRECT FORM of "Table" and for the "Correct" Tribes to be Seated at it.

~~~

Day 13:

03.29.2020

The THREE-legged stool of CHANGE: biology, economy, sociology:

-666 inverted is 999: temperature reported for Covid19—99.9 degrees

-99.9% Income Disparity in 2020 (Note: 06.14.2020 Gold Fineness "PURE" = 999.9).

-Following George Floyd Public Lynching: President Trump and GOP states, "99.9%" of police are "good" apples; "No Systemic Racism" (aka Institutionalized Racism).

-Mark of the Beast Symbolism in the Time of a Tribulation, 2020, is supported by the fact that in this time we, colloquially, call "Misinformation" literally means a time in which deception and manipulation are Normal. Good is bad/bad is good. Love is hate/hate is love. Kindness is cruelty/cruelty is kindness—these Truths confirm that we are, in fact, in a Tribulation. It is further confirmed by the fact that even when the Truth is revealed (a Herculean feat in a Time of Misinformation) it is not "HEARD".

-99.9 Frequency: thanks to poverty I was deprived of internet. Necessity for Music made me dig out my old radio but Covid-19 made me curious to discover meaning so I decided to "dial in" 99.9 where I heard country music, 1980s music, and Seattle rock—all fun—but it made me ponder what Radio symbolizes that TV/Internet CAN'T? Listening ONLY. Plus it's MegaHertz (MHz).

-Megahertz: one MILLION hertz; radio transmission frequency; computer clock speed (frequency and SPEED of microprocessors); it is USAGE OVER TIME; began in WORLD WAR TWO; named after Heinrich Rudolf Hertz (1857-**1894)** the first person to provide CONCLUSIVE PROOF of ELECTROMAGNETIC WAVES (Note: Recall US history Timeline of 1894). Most common uses of Megahertz: Sine Waves and MUSICAL TONES (See: The Living Song Project/the Optimistic American: Voir Dire). In German, "Herz" means HEART. In Christian Apologetics this means: "Christians, REMOVE ENTIRELY your OWN CORRUPTED and FAILING HEART with that of Christ's RIGHT THIS MINUTE! You have wasted ALL the Time ALLOTTED YOU. The "clock" began when the First Angel of David's Seven arrived, 2020. Christians, become Christ's Heart NOW or be utterly destroyed. It is YOUR FREE WILL—your CHOICES—it always has been."

~~~

Day 12:

1)

"Planetary Defenders Validate Asteroid Deflection Code," Nolan O'Brien et al, 03.27.2020, phys.org; Lawrence Livermore National Laboratory (LLNL)/Tané Remington, Earth and Space Science; Modeling Plan; DART (double asteroid redirection test); modeling system used for simulation; first ever KINETIC impact deflection demonstration on a NEAR-EARTH Asteroid; DART spacecraft will DELIBERATELY CRASH into the smaller MOONLET in the binary asteroid (ETA09.2022) ; using Baseline Data Collected 1991 Kyoto University; BASALT sphere target; DART spacecraft (ETA07.2021); ASSUMED FACTOR—Basalt; TARGET: Binary Asteroid (two asteroids orbiting each other) named DIDYMUS (nickname: Didymoon).

2)

Didymus is St. Judas Thomas the Apostle (the Doubter). The Gnostic Gospels of Thomas are DENIED by modern Canonical Leaders; it is said that Thomas was Jesus of Nazarene's twin.

3)

Didymus, Ancient Greek Dídyma, means "Twin, double, twin brother"; Didyma is an Ancient Greek SANCTUARY on the Coast of IONIA—contained temple and oracle of Apollo, the Didymaion; Theodora and Didymus are Christian Saints; Astrologically, Gemini is "twins" in Latin, located in Northern hemisphere, 1 of 48 constellations described by the 2nd Century AD Astronomer, PTOLEMY, Greek mythology of Castor & Pollux, lies between Taurus and Cancer.

4)

Prior to 1990 summer Solstice (first day of the Summer Season)—in Classical Antiquity—Cancer NOT Gemini was the location of the SUN; during the 1st Centuray AD the SUN SHIFTED TO GEMINI; in 1990 the sun shifted, again, and will REMAIN IN TAURUS until the 27th Century AD (when it shifts to Aries—the extreme).

5)

The Ancient Library of Alexandria, Egypt: one of the largest and most significant libraries of the ANCIENT world, part of the research institute named MOUSEION dedicated to the MUSES (the NINE Goddesses of ARTS); Myth: burned once then cataclysmically destroyed—part of the library was burned by JULIUS Caesar during his Civil War (48 BC) but the Library of Alexandria, Egypt declined gradually over the course of several centuries STARTING WITH THE PURGING of INTELLECTUALS from Alexandria (145BC) during the reign of PTOLEMY Physcon VIII (182 BC-116 BC) which resulted in a DIASPORA of scholarship.

6)

Ptolemy—a common name in the Upper Class during the time of Alexander the Great (several named Ptolemy are in his army); Claudius Ptolemy (born 100AD) was a 2nd Century Alexandrian astronomer, mathematician, geographer, and astrologer; Alexandria/Roman province of Egypt under rule of Roman Empire; 9th century Persian Astronomer, Abu Ma'shar—Ptolemy was a member of Egypt's ROYAL lineage, considered Wise; Ptolemy wrote, "HARMONICS" on the Mathematics of Music called PYTHAGOREAN TUNING.

7)

The Pythagoreans, the Dangerous Ratio, and the Murder of Hippasus for discovering the Inconvenient Truth of the number, 0 (zero/null/nil) that would eventually form the bases of a new language, Code (010101)

~~~

Day 11:

03.27.2020

I.

Question: What are the neurological implications of Sars-CoV-2 (Covid-19)?

II.

Google Scholar search: brain stimulation, god experience. Results: #1) 1983, "Religious and mystical experience as ARTIFACTS of the TEMPORAL LOBE FUNCTION: a general hypothesis"; #2) 2010, "The Spiritual Doorway in the Brain: A Neurologist's Search for God Experience" indicating a strong involvement by the LIMBIC SYSTEM; #3) 2008, Ballantine Books, "Why God Won't Go Away: Brain Science and the Biology of Belief" using SPECT, observing brain at peak meditative state, noted, "Unusual activity in a small lump of gray matter nestled in the top rear section of the brain—a highly SPECIALIZED BUNDLE OF NEURONS," in the posterior superior parietal lobe, a part of the brain that allows us to distinguish between the INDIVIDUAL and EVERYTHING ELSE.

III.

"Severe Acute Respiratory Syndrome Coronavirus infection causes NEURONAL DEATH in the absence of encephalitis in mice transgenic for HUMAN ACE2," Journal of Virology 82(15) 2008; "Brain infection may result in LONG-TERM NEUROLOGICAL Sequelae, but little is known about the pathogenesis of Sars-CoV in THIS organ." Search: is limbic system close to olfactory bulb—result: olfactory bulb IS ONE OF THE STRUCTURES OF THE LIMBIC SYSTEM; the olfactory bulb is connected to the HYPTHALAMIC NUCLEI which connects to the AMYGDALOID BODY: the limbic system TRANSLATES sensory date from the NEO-CORTEX (our Thinking Brain) into MOTIVATIONAL FORCES FOR BEHAVIOR & ACTION (source: Texas School for the Blind); Nucleus Amygdalae (a function: emotion); Septum Pellucidum, a sheet/double membrane separation running from corpus collosum to fornix, anterior horns of left and right ventricles (a function other than as a PHYSICAL BARRIER is NOT WELL UNDERSTOOD); source: Magnetic Resonance Imaging in Obstetrics, 2018—"During fetal development the SEPTUM PELLUCIDEM is filled with CSF (cerebrospinal fluid) and is referred to as the 'cavum septi pellucidum'"; pathway of Olfactory Bulb: Cranial Nerve 1-CNI/1 of 12 cranial nerves; one of the FEW CRANIAL NERVES THAT CARRIES SPECIAL SENSORY INFORMATION ONLY (unlike cells associated with other special senses like vision or hearing cells associated with receiving OLFACTORY information can REGENERATE THROUGOUT LIFE ("regenerative capable cells", biologically speaking, have "potential" for help and for harm); other cell types present in the epithelium: BASAL

STEM CELLS; Olfactory Cortex is not a single structure, it is defined as the combined areas of the cerebral cortex that RECEIVE INPUT DIRECTLY from the Olfactory Bulb; the Olfactory Cortex includes: Piriform Cortex, AMYGDALA (housing EMOTION/FEAR), Entorhinal Cortex or the PARAHIPPOCAMPAL GYRUS (houses the FORMATION OF MEMORY); Source: Kenhub serving 1,333,876 anatomy students: Clinical implications of ANOSMIA (loss of smell): associated with NEUROLOGICAL DEGENERATIVE DISEASE such as: Alzheimer's, schizophrenia, DIABETES, Huntington's disease, Multiple Sclerosis, Pick's disease (a form of dementia), Parkinson's disease (anosmia often precedes motor change), and from brain injuries from tumor/aneurism or trauma also DYSOSMIA (parosmia/troposmia/cacosmia and phantosmia or olfactory "hallucination."

Hypotheses: 1) Covid-19, via the Olfactory Pathway through the Limbic System (ablation of smell, hallucination, homeostasis interruption) onto the Spinal Cord (antibodies found in CSF) may affect a person's "experience" of "god"/God and 2) Covid-19 will have SIGNIFICANT EFFECT on how we "experience" our world from cradle to grave—because ALL things (drugs and disease) capable of traversing barriers (blood-brain and placental) always have, historically. What to look for with fetuses exposed, in utero, to Covid-19: agenesis/hypogenesis of Corpus Collosum (congenital malformation).

~~~

Day 10:

03.27.2020

The Abomination of Desolation and the Futurist's (Futurism Christianity) View of Holistic Propriety—

I.

Sermon on the Mount: anglicized from the Matthew/Vulgate chapters 5-7 (note: sabattical—7; Jubillee—5(10)), Latin, section title "Sermo in Monte"; collection of sayings and teachings of Jesus Christ; emphasis on his Moral Teaching; OCCURS EARLY IN CHRIST'S MINISTRY but after Christ's 1) Baptism 2) 40 day fast and temptation from Satan and 3) he'd begun to preach in Galilee; it is the LONGEST CONTINUOUS DISCOURSE OF JESUS FOUND IN THE NEW TESTAMENT; it is the MOST WIDELY QUOTED element of the CANONICAL GOSPELS and includes 1) Beatitudes 2) Lord's Prayer and 3) the BEST KNOWN TEACHINGS OF CHRIST; the Sermon on the Mount is generally considered to contain the CENTRAL TENETS OF CHRISTIAN DISCIPLESHIP.

II.

First Published in 1956 (first English translation: 1977) The Gospel of Thomas is very different in tone and structure from other New Testament Apocrypha and the FOUR Canonical Gospels; it is a NARRATIVE account of Jesus; it consists of Logia (sayings) attributed to Jesus; sometimes a stand alone; sometimes embedded in short dialogues or parables; referred to as a "SAYINGS GOSPEL"; some suggest it is evidence of a "Q SOURCE" (material drawn from the Early Church's ORAL TRADITION); according to Mark, Thomas is regarded as the TWIN BROTHER OF JESUS (See: biology's chimera + physic's Banach-Tarski Paradox); the Gospel of Thomas proclaims, in Saying 113, that the Kingdom of God is ALREADY PRESENT FOR THOSE WHO UNDERSTAND THE SECRET MESSAGE OF JESUS (See: Tolstoy's "The Kingdom of God is Within You" + Buddhism's enlightenment through skillful meditation); the Gospel of Thomas LACKS APOCALYPTIC THEMES; Bart Ehrman argues, "The Gospel of Thomas was, probably, composed by a GNOSTIC sometime in the early SECOND CENTURY (see: Ptolemy); considered by some as one of the EARLIEST ACCOUNTS OF THE TEACHINGS OF JESUS; no MAJOR Christian group ACCEPTS this Gospel as Canonical or Authoritative; modern scholars do not believe it was written by the Apostle Thomas (modernity having taken up the mantle of the "Doubter").

III.

Gnostic—Ancient Greek—"having KNOWLEDGE"; ancient religions, ideas and systems; 1st century AD; EARLY Christians AND Jews; emphasized "PERSONAL SPIRITUAL KNOWLEDGE" (gnosis); refused orthodox teachings, traditions, and ecclesiastical AUTHORITY; many Gnostic texts deal with ILLUSION AND ENLIGHTENMENT; many Gnostic texts DO NOT focus on Sin & Repentance; *FATHERS* OF THE EARLY CURCH DENOUCED THEM AS *HERETICS*.

IV.

To my ignorant eye—they're all saying the same damned thing: LOVE! Canon, no canon. Plagiarism, no plagiarism. You say, Pota-to, I say Po-tato—neither recognize the written word, "Poetaytow" but we both enjoy sharing a meal of the brown object we dug out of the earth, which is, in Reality, the same fucking TUBER!

~~~

Day 9:

Friday, 3/27/2020

A)

Question: Why is the "mark" of the "Beast" (666) so specific? Covid-19 (a chimera; mythologically, a chimera is a woman) threshold temperature: 99.9 degrees; the Biblical 666 predates the invention of thermometers; Therm is Greek for "Heat" or "Warm"; Tribulation in the "Church" Era (note: Capital Ministries (the Church of President Donald J. Trump's Administration) states that the Coronavirus CAN'T be God's Wrath for anything EXCEPT 'reaping and sowing' because of "HOMOSEXUALITY and ABORTION"); Tribulation is defined as a cause of GREAT trouble or suffering ["MAKE" (aka force) "America GREAT" (greatness, like any tool, can be for good or evil) "again" (revealing the DESIRE for reconstruction of America's past or REGRESSION) and the "Silent" Christians delivered the Heart of Christ to be executed in THIS SPIRIT OF THE TIME (Zeitgeist) no differently than those who ABUSED THEIR POWER (religious and political) when Christ FIRST CAME—and the "Christians" (Christ's Jewish Disciples and adherents/followers/fans) REMAINED SILENT as the Messiah was TORTURED/PUBLICALLY HUMILIATED and Executed on the Public "Square" (the "crossroad" for travelers—business, personal, religious—would not be ABLE TO TRAVERSE WITHOUT BECOMING A WITNESS to the "FRUITS" of Corruption (socially engineered oppression, socially enabled injustice, and collectively assigned consequence of participating—willingly, wittingly, of an Innocent's murder—for if one does NOTHING, says NOTHING, one has ACTED and IS COMPLICIT; we can try to "refuse" this responsibility, telling ourselves, "It wasn't me," but if your voice hasn't become MUTED from PROTESTATION AGAINST CORRUPTION…then you will carry responsibility for corruption as far as you are part of a Corrupt Collective); DJT'S Capital Minister said that, in the "Church Era" God won't bring destruction like in the Old Testament "until Tribulation" but he is SURE this can't be Tribulation (2020).

B)

Christian Eschatology: the Great Tribulation (Revelation 7:14; Matthew 24: 21, 29); Biblical 144,000 Jews become missionaries (Jews for Jesus) believed to be Jewish Christians, sealed for deliverance from the Destruction of Jerusalem in 70AD; Revelation 7:14|Matthew 24:21, 29 The Great Tribulation—mistakenly Christian DISPENSATIONALISTS believe the Tribulation (End of Times) occurs BEFORE Christ's Second Coming.

C)

Spiritual Hypothesis: The Tribulation IS TRIGGERED BY Christ's RETURN—the King inspects His troops, witnesses his Body's Heresy and Blasphemy, takes note (makes a List and checks it TWICE) of who, individually AND collectively, INVOKE HIS FATHER'S NAME FOR CORRUPT PURPOSE; The Tribulation is what we will ENDURE for FAILING (and continuing to SPECTACULARLY FAIL for two thousand fucking years!) to CARRY OUT OUR ORDERS TO TRANSPLANT OUR HEARTS for Christ's Heart so we could BEGIN THE GREAT WORK of creating God's World in Christ's IMAGE.

~~~

Day 8:

1)

The Wisdom of Equal Treatment: Apply the Trump Administration "Zero Tolerance" principle…to ALL Administrations—regarding Corruption; all people or businesses who EMPLOY "illegal" immigrants will SUFFER THE SAME LEGAL CONSEQUENCES as the the "Illegal" does when the ICE AGENTS COME FOR THEM—in other words, "Do unto others as you would HAVE them do unto you;" I imagine the positional "rubber necking" or "flip flopping" for holding such INTOLERANCE would be measured in NANOSECONDS if those who propose regressive/punitive/Draconian measures apply to "special" or "other" people REALIZED they also, EQUALLY, apply to themselves.

2)

03.25.2020 I describe, in my unscientific mind, Sars-CoV-2 (Covid-19) as a "hybrid"; Alexandre Hassanin, the conversation, sciencealert.com, 12.2019, genus Rhinolophus, bat (cave)/pangolin (forest), intermediate host—palm civet/paguma larvata (host in between bat & human); 96% genome identical (concordance); bats constitute reservoir of SarsCov, specifically Rhinophus; 27 of the 41 hospitalized (66%) Wuhan, China; betacoronavirus Sars-CoV-2 is close to SarsCoV (11/2002) spread to 29 countries—total 8,098/774 deaths.

3)

02.07.2020 Discovered in Malaysian pangolin (Manis Javanica) only 90% genome—virus isolated in Pangolin NOT responsible for Covid-19; Pangolin was 99% in a specific region of the S protein which corresponds to the 74 amino acids involved in the ACE receptor binding domain—the one that ALLOWS the virus to enter human cells to infect them (Question: how would SarsCoV2 infected cells respond to ACE inhibition meds used for cardiovascular disorder?) "ACE" refers to the hormone, angiotensin converting enzyme 2 that may, in addition to locally exertion of affect in the kidneys, act on the central nervous system; bat (intermediate horseshoe bat or R. Affinis/RaTG13) is highly DIVERGENT in this SPECIFIC region (77% similarity) which means coronavirus isolated from pangolin is capable of entering human cells—it is less clear (22% less) how effectively coronavirus isolated from R. Affinis (bats) can.

4)

Genomic comparisons suggest that SarsCoV2 is a RECOMBINATION between TWO DIFFERENT VIRUSES—one clase to RaTG13 and the other closer to the pangolin virus. "In other words it is a CHIMERA between TWO PRE-EXISTING VIRUSES."

5)

Chimera—Greek mythology—fire breathing female monster with a Lion's head, a Goat's body, and a Serpent's (or Dragon's) tail; Biologically: a chimera is an organism containing a mixture of genetically different tissues, formed by the process such as FUSION of EARLY EMBRYOS,

GRAFTING, OR MUTATION—there ARE Human Chimeras (100 reported cases) who possess TWO TOTALLY DIFFERENT SETS OF DNA INSIDE THEIR BODY (11/2017).

~~~

Day 7:

"The Family" & their "Cyrus/Wolf leader/king" and America's Denial of Christ 3 times (as did the Apostle Paul; both with the SAME outcome for the World):

1st cock's crow:

Thanksgiving, 2019—"I am the Chosen One," President Donald John Trump proclaimed, looking up to Heaven. In broad daylight, by word AND DEED, he proclaimed himself Christ the Messiah. American Christians remained, overwhelmingly, silent and those who did speak did not proclaim and declare, "HERESY!"

2nd cock's crow:

Easter, 2020—with professed Christian leader standing beside him, President Donald John Trump invoked the Divinity of Easter without ONE MENTION OF CHRIST! The Christians surrounding him REFUSED TO MENTION THE NAME OF THEIR OWN LORD AND SAVIOR; they remained silent.

3rd cock's crow:

George Floyd Lynching & the "Cyrus/Wolf" king's Bible as Theatrical Property (see Biblical definition of Hypocrite): if Christ had just been crucified in the American streets "this" Cyrus would grab the Cross and would use ALL his strength to prop it up just long enough to get the "snap" before letting it drop to ground for if he would hold up a book he's never read, standing before a community's body he never nurtures, while ordering innocent people to be brutalized so he could "create an image of himself—to his 'likeness'" then I have no doubt, he'd get a picture of himself holding the wooden cross used to execute the Son of God: it's what ALL "Trophy Hunters" do.

On this final, this third cock's crow, *some* Christians answered; may the Pauls among you now go forth with an indwelled Heart of Christ to Repair the Breach…for we are in the time of Wolves and our King *is* coming.

American Christians—you have forgotten YOUR HYMNS! "We are one in the Spirit, we are ONE in the Lord, and we pray that OUR UNITY will one day be RESTORED, we will WORK WITH EACH OTHER WE WILL WORK SIDE BY SIDE, and they'll KNOW we are Christians by our LOVE, by our Love, yes they'll know we are Christians by our love."

But the line of that beautiful hymn—that TRUTHFUL hymn of Wisdom—that is often forgotten, "We'll GUARD **EACH** MAN'S DIGNITY and SAVE EACH MAN'S PRIDE." I only add the caveat: "each person's dignity, each person's pride" for it is time for the CORRUPTION OF MISOGYNY, like RACISM, and all other "intolerance" to immediately, upon this notice, cease and desist.

~~~

Day 6:

03.25.2020 @ 04:05-04:19 Thomas Sowell, "Basic Economics: A common Sense Guide to Economy," youtube, basic economics, Thomas Sowell, audible audio edition: 1) "The underlying principles involved in most economic events are usually not very complicated in themselves. Basic principles apply around the world and throughout history but the political rhetoric and economic jargon which by which they are discussed can make those events seem murky." 2) @ 05:15 "What is an economy? The GARDEN OF EDEN was a system of the production of goods and services but it was NOT an economy. WITHOUT SCARCITY there is NO NEED TO ECONOMIZE because there is NO NEED, everything was available in UNILIMITED ABUNDANce."

My observation: Sowell (noting his introductory use of loaded language like "heathen") is CONFLATING "relative deprivation" and Disparity Consciousness with literal/actual deprivation. Constraint is conflated with "want" vs. "need." He conflates "scarcity" with "wants." @ 09:00, after muddling the above terms, he further, erroneously, qualifies that to overcome *scarcity* people must "satisfy ALL our DESIRES to the FULLEST."

Words matter. Precision matters. Our Intellectuals must be as ETHICAL as ALL who are entrusted with POWER. A man of his education and prestige knows damned well the effect of parsing—and he CHOSE to do it anyway. Shame on him and all my fellow Intellectuals who've allowed their BIAS to CORRUPT objective Reality.

~~~

Day 5:

Ponderings:

A.

03.23.2020 Covid-19 lives longer on plastic than metal (specifically copper), glass, and natural fiber (cardboard)—good thing even the breastmilk of Wealthy Women is inundated with microplastics...I'm sure it will ALL work out just fine.

B.

03.23.2020 Thou shalt NOT KILL (OT God was pretty "precise" in His commands, didn't seem interested in Loopholes); Abel pleased God most because he offered his BEST and did it WITHOUT KILLING (he was a farmer not a rancher, in other words he harvested sewn seed) and Cain, who did NOT give his "best" bull to be sacrificed (believing it best to keep the best bull for breeding with the hope of producing greater numbers of better bulls—he was a rancher) and God was DISPLEASED because Cain offered TO GOD—second best. But God, loving ALL his children, didn't "kill" Cain on the spot…he reprimanded his MISUNDERSTANDING, and Cain, not appreciating being reprimanded (think Pride, Hubris, Bias) decided that HIS BEST COURSE OF ACTION WAS TO KILL…not the bull he was SUPPOSED to "kill" as A SACRIFICE TO GOD…but his brother. (Yes I realize the hypocrisy of "do not kill" but Cain gets shit for NOT killing—but it is because the act of killing itself creates psychological/emotional/spiritual SCHISM (or Self pain and suffering), which means that if Cain had been willing to ENDURE the PERSONAL PAIN & SUFFERING caused within himself in the form of a Schism by committing the ACT OF KILLING out of REVERENCE and DUTY to God—then his sacrifice would have been as pleasing as Abel's (who, unlike Cain, was blessed NOT to have to kill to be able to offer a Pleasing Sacrifice of HIS best). Cain didn't lose God's favor because he killed his brother but because he offered God something LESS THAN HIS BEST and VICTIMIZED "HIS" OWN SOUL (which, victimizes the Image of God within as well—for what is done to the Least…what we do to ourselves we do to God within us) and then he goes and murders his brother—because he refused to become REPENTENT for "his" original sin. (Note: Covid-19 was declared a global pandemic on March 11, 2020; section B was written on 12 days later—"By April 23 (2020), there were more than 3,400 reported positive cases (Covid-19) in meatpacking facilities in 62 plants in 23 states." Source: "Mapping Covid-19 in meat and food processing plants," Food and Environment Reporting Network. 2020-04-22.

C.

03.20.2020 The phrase, "Do not judge" has been corrupted (like Sowell's economic terms) and now, colloquially and in Christianity, to mean, "do not criticize or evaluate." Ask people of color (especially women) what that means in an oppressive system (clue: keep your mouth shut, stay in your lane, be invisible—seen not heard—and don't "bitch"). To take this approach of not judging, not criticizing or evaluating, makes as much sense, spiritually, as saying to a Covid-19 patient, "I won't tell you your symptoms or what—in my professional opinion and experience— might be the BEST WAY FORWARD FOR YOU because I don't want you to feel I'm 'judging' you." When a "body" is sick (infected) we need the RIGHT kind of DOCTOR to tell the TRUTH even if it's inconvenient and UNWELCOMED. For Christians this means you must listen to the Christian Reformers who will HELP YOU to PROPERLY DIAGNOSE what is KILLING THE BODY of Christ. It is His church. It is His body. His HEART is the Life-saving PRESCRIPTION American Christians need—and, without it, the Body perishes no differently than a biologic body riddled with the MOST VIRULENT cancer.

~~~

Day 4:

03.18.2020 Parable of the CD Player's Foot: because of financial insecurity (increased costs without increased budget) not everyone in my family has a cell phone—we share. This means when my husband has the phone I can't listen to music, which I love and listen to daily. So I dug out my old CD/Radio boombox. I could still enjoy the music—still have my "need" met—even through the annoyance of static interference and commercials; I was very thankful, especially knowing there are so many others in the world who go without ACTUAL NEEDS…what is static compared to a pinching of a starving stomach—answer: NOTHING! My "needs" are trivial (though my needs are not any less trivial or more important than those of ALL my fellow Living Beings). Wisdom came when I noticed, pretty quickly, that the CD player "wobbled" when I touched it; it was not shored up properly so I put a piece of cardboard, a WEDGE, under where I thought it was "off" but it didn't work so I flipped it over (accepting the risk that such "rough" handling might injure the mechanism) and learned that all but ONE of the original four "foot" pads were missing. I picked at it with my fingernail but it would not budge. I got a butter-knife from the kitchen but every time it skipped across the pad's surface—it took a few tries before realizing the tip was too big to do the job. Before my husband had to stop practicing as a physical therapist, when we still owned and operated our own business (a small clinic), we had a metal letter opener to process the mail—I got it and its pointed tip did the trick; basic scientific method: hypothesize, test, based on results A) reject hypothesis or B) affirm and retest.

Moral of the story: sometimes it all comes down to evaluating available tools and determining—QUICKLY BUT ACCURATELY—which is BEST SUITED to the TASK AT HAND.

~~~

Day 3:

03.17.2020

$

Questions: Is this the Second Coming of the Angel of Death? Were the previous wars/pestilence/famines but Reflections of our the Failure of our Own Spirit? How many times must____ … ?

Ponderings: "The answer, My friend, is blowing in the wind"(ow)…old saying, "Open the wind(ow)—in-flew-enza" (aka influenza); Legalistic Christians attribute all disease (but especially sexually transmitted disease) to "immorality"—I wonder how these same Legalistic Christians explain the deaths of faithful Christians all over the world from Covid-19.

¢

03.17.2020 "Spring is coming EARLIER this year than it has since **1896**. The vernal (spring) equinox—which means the beginning of spring in the Northern Hemisphere—will take place on the Thursday, March 19 throughout the ENTIRE UNITED STATES, including Alaska and Hawaii. This is EARLIER THAN ANY OTHER EQUINOX IN THE LAST 124 YEARS." Accuweather said; The equinox usually falls either on March 20 or 21. "The complicated reasons for 2020's earlier equinox include: Leap Years (see: manmade), Centuries (see: manmade), and length of time it takes Earth to revolve around the sun (see: something-greater-than-made)," cbs.news said—the equinox, which takes place @ 11:50PM Thursday is the PRECISE MOMENT the sun's rays shine DIRECTLY ON THE EQUATOR (10:50PM CDT, 9:50PM MDT, 8:50 PM PDT); Thursday will be one of the TWO days out of the year—the other being the day of the Autumnal Equinox in SEPTEMBER—when the Earth's axis is tilted NEITHER toward nor away from the Sun, resulting in ROUGHLY TWELVE HOURS of daylight and 12 HRS of DARKNESS ALMOST EVERYWHERE ON EARTH." (See the Nature of Equality); word Equinox originated from 2 Latin words 1) aequus (equal) and 2) nox (night).

$

Meteorologists define seasons differently—as of March 1ˢᵗ, 2020 NYT Top News: #1) "Winning South Carolina, Biden Makes Case Against Sanders"; #2) "Trump Moves To Calm Fears As FIRST US DEATH From Coronovirus is Reported"; #3) "Taliban and US Strike Deal to Withdraw American Troops from Afghanistan."

¢

Equinox is also one of the TWO days each year when almost every spot on the Earth—except the Poles (geographical extremities) "experience" a SUNRISE DUE EAST and a SUNSET DUE WEST; It is my belief that, in 2020, this is a prophetic metaphor; headline, Editor's pick, "For Seoul's Poor, Class Strife in *Parasite* (SEE: the movie) is Daily Reality." Joseph Campbell (1904-1987), "The cave you fear to enter holds the treasure you seek," 05.23.2013.

$

Shakespeare, King Lear, was written while sequestered during a Plague outbreak.

¢

1896: Presidential election William McKinley (R); R defeated D (in 2020 same two-party system/fully inverted); William Jennings Bryan (D), orator, Nebraska, US House of Rep, Sec. of State under Woodrow Wilson, because of his faith in the Wisdom of the Common People he was often called THE GREAT COMMONER, attacked the teaching of Evolution in the SCOPES trial (Scopes trail is the PIVOT POINT), attacked Gold Standard in "Cross of Gold Speech," elected by the Left-Wing POPULIST PARTY; Events of 1896, Europe: 10/1896, Winston Churchill is transferred to Bombay, India, 09.24.1986 F. Scott Fitzgerald is born (Irish descent),

Salome premiers in Paris, rehearsals for plays' debut on London Stage began in 1892 but were HALTED when the Lord Chamberlain's licensor of plays BANNED *Salome* on the basis that it was ILLEGAL TO DEPICT BIBLICAL CHARACTERS ON THE STAGE, *1896 Swedish Scientist SVANTE ARRHENIUS QUANTIFIES CARBON DIOXIDE'S ROLE IN WARMING THE EARTH*; 1896, US: William "Buffalo Bill" Cody FOUNDS the City of Cody, Wyoming, 01.16.1896 1st Un-Official college basketball game, U. of Iowa, UTAH is the 45th STATE admitted to the union (vote was 31,305 to 7,607); 1896—Final Ruling on Plessy v. Ferguson

$

The Tragedy of Two Spectacles (a Tsar's and a Crush Texan's) 1896:

I.) 05.18.1896 Khondynka Tragedy: Nicholas II crowned Tsar of Russia on 05.14.1896, 4 days later: 150 buffets with gifts/20 pubs built, evening of 05.17.1896 people heard RUMORs of gifts from the Tsar (gifts of: a/one bread roll, a piece of sausage, pretzels, gingerbread, and a mug), by 5AM (on 05.18.1896), according to Jay Leyda, 500,000 had gathered, RUMOR OF SHORTAGE, 1,800 police FAILED TO MAINTAIN ORDER, PANIC—1,384 TRAMPLED TO DEATH—Firsthand account of Khondynka Tragedy: "The parties, receptions, and balls following the coronation were DARKENED by the CATASTROPHE at Khondynka, where 2,000 people were CRUSHED TO DEATH. The same day as the catastrophe, I was taking a walk along the Khondinka and I met MANY GROUPS OF PEOPLE COMNG BACK FROM THE SITE and carrying the Tsar's gifts. The strange thing, though, was that NOT ONE PERSON MENTIONED THE CATASTROPHE, and I did not hear about it until the NEXT MORNING at the Government General's PALACE, where General Prefect of Police, VLASOVKSI, brought a special report. Grand Duke, SERGE ALEXANDROVICH, was very depressed by what had happened; he gave Vlasovski orders to return to him every hour with detailed reports on the progress of the INVESTIGATION INTO THE CAUSES OF THE DISASTER." Source: Memories of Alexei Volkov.

II.) 09.15.1896 Crush, Texas: Crush, Texas was a temporary "city" established as a ONE-DAY PUBLICITY STUNT to publically demonstrate a "Train Wreck" by William George Crush of the Missouri-Kansas-Texas Railroad (popularly known as, "Katy"), 40,000 people, police moved people to what they "believed" to be "safe" distance, photographer JARUS "Joe" DEAN LOST HIS EYE to a flying bolt, when the engine BOILERS UNEXPECTEDLY EXPLODED discharged debris HUNDREDS OF FEET INTO THE AIR; Killed 3: 2 YOUNG men and 1 Woman; 6 seriously injured, spectators turned and ran in BLIND PANIC "People ran in TERROR" "The trains themselves were COMPLETELY DESTROYED, except for their last cars, which remained, virtually, untouched." "After the crowd RECOVERED from the BLAST, it

SWARMED OVER THE WRECKAGE TO FIND SOUVENIRS." (See Vultures and the wolves of Valkyries: I) in Greek mythology the Vulture is the descendent of the Griffin and held SACRED to the MOTHER/Maternal GODDDESS ISIS II) in Norse mythology Valkyries are the lovers of Heroes (bringing them sex & mead when they are not needed in the battle of Ragnarok/Tribulation), described as daughters of Royalty, sometimes accompanied by Ravens, Swans, Horses—with a variant, Sigrún—"the troll-woman's mount"—being connected to wolves'; "It was the rarest and strongest of woman Formed of northern snow and gold Odin's daughter sword of FIRE A Valkyrie," wiki).

¢

03.17.2020 Even as a bird-brain mirrors its behavior in front of a mirror, our actions create mirrored action, which is meant to SHOW or REVEAL TO us what WE LOOK LIKE and HOW we're BEHAVING. Mirror neurons were never meant to be used as WEAPONS (used as tools of manipulation by CORRUPTION) it was meant to be a TOOL FOR EMPATHY so that we could FINALLY EXPERIENCE real and GENUINE AFFECT FOR OUR ACTION/INACTION…so that, by our own BRAIN, we "feel" what we're ACTUALLY doing to others by PERSONALLY FEELING the HARM directly and indirectly resulting from "what I have done and by what I have left UNDONE"; in a Material World you can dress a person in the finest fashion, with a cadre accentuating "asset" while "hiding liability" (physical flaw) but that person will NEVER be as BEAUTIFUL as those who DISPLAY BEAUTY by BEING beautiful—those who display, through ACTION, a LOVING SOUL are the MOST EXQUISITLEY LOVELY AND DESIRABLE CREATURES ON THIS PLANET! Truth; 05.14.2020 Vision: a massive, all consuming "Fire" prompted the question, "How to build a fire shelter?" 05.13.2020 the answer preceded the question: "Emancipate yourself from Mental Slavery" and I rejoiced at the Wisdom of Jubilee: the 50th year is when the SLAVES ARE FREED AND LANDS LOST TO DEBT ARE RETURNED TO THEIR ORIGINAL OWNERS. Amen!

~~~

Day 2:

The Wisdom of an 18-Year Old "Woman's" Abduction & Rape:

I.

Miranda: "You have the RIGHT to REMAIN Silent. Anything you SAY can and WILL be used AGAINST YOU in a Court of law."

II.

March 2, 1963: an 18-year old Phoenix, AZ woman reports she'd been abducted, driven to the desert, and raped to the POLICE. Detectives gave HER A POLYGRAPH but the tests were "inconclusive" (See: testing reliability of polygraph). They TRACKED THE LICENSE PLATE NUMBER OF THE CAR (Note: good job 18-year old "woman" who'd been traumatized by abduction and rape to be ABLE to recall a license plate number! That is more than MANY women can do under conditions of TORTURE; Aside: I used quotations on the word woman because she was only 18 years old and often our male military soldiers are called, colloquially, "boys" especially for the rhetorical effect of claiming the horror of war, for example "Our *boys* are dying over there." It is rhetorical manipulation for if it is "boys" in the horror of war and it is a "woman" in the horror of abduction/rape…it creates an artificial "maturation" through use of SPECIFIC LANGUAGE.)

*Note: if you want to know whether or not our Law is misogynistic—this "woman/girl" who was TORTURED, who had the ABILITY to not only SURVIVE TORTURE but to remember a license plate—this AMAZING WOMAN—and the "law" BORN FROM HER RAPE is named after the man who raped her…it is HIS name, Ernesto **Miranda**, that ALL COPS PROCLAIM EVERY TIME THEY ARREST MEN AND WOMEN AND CHILDREN. She has been erased, altogether, but his name—the PERPETRATOR's—has been historically preserved and "recited" every day as if a prayer.

June 13th 1966—the U.S. Supreme Court hands down its decision in **MIRANDA** v. ARIZONA.

(Note: Sheriff Joe Arpaio's [Maricopa County, AZ] Presidential Pardon by Donald J. Trump (the 45th) after he'd been CONVICTED of the CRIME of CRIMINAL CONTEMPT OF COURT—though a criminal misdemeanor the DISRESPECT DISPLAYED TOWARDS THE COURT he was ENTRUSTED BY THE PUBLIC TO PROTECT AND DEFEND is indefensibly corrosive to FAITH IN INSTITUTIONAL JUSTICE.)

The driving purpose behind Miranda Rights is to PREVENT LAW ENFORCEMENT from FORCING individuals being INTERROGATED to INCRIMINATE themselves (a person's RIGHT against COMPELLED self-incrimination is HOUSED in the 5th Amendment of the Constitution and upheld in the 6th—the RIGHT to counsel).

III.

We are the Silent Sentinels of 2020. The Women's War of 2020. 150 years—what FRUIT? 10% of women REFUSE to have children—we go extinct as a species; "It's not nice to FOOL MOTHER NATURE," said the 1977 Chiffon margarine commercial; the 1980 Enjoli perfume commercial, "I can bring home the bacon, fry it up in a pan, and never ever let you forget you're a man 'cause I'm a woman"; or the 1971 KEEP AMERICA BEAUTIFUL "Crying Indian" commercial Iron Eyes Cody (Italian American actor, Espera de Corti) starred in while dressed in traditional Native American artifact as he cries and the narrator states, "Some people have a deep, abiding RESPECT for the NATURAL BEAUTY THAT WAS ONCE THIS Country. And

SOME "people" don't." (See: Citizens United and Legal establishment of a corporation's "right" to be a "person" with certain legal privileges the same as biologic people but without **complete legal liability** of biologic people).

Propaganda is Propaganda is Propaganda ad infinitum—which is why we must, when we speak at all, tell the Truth, the Whole Truth, and NOTHING but the Truth…because propaganda, whether for "good" intention or "bad" is still manipulation—and that is CONTRARY TO FREE WILL (one can't be free in one's will if one's will is conditioned…that's still SLAVERY).

So although the "messages" of the commercials above scratch the itch of my personal bias (align with my personal worldview) the fact that those with GOOD INTENTION had been, for TOO LONG, managed through APPEASEMENT resulting in neither lasting nor adequate CHANGE…led to those with Wisdom as to how to MOVE FORWARD WITHOUT EXTINCTION…resorted to the methods of the Oppressors—manipulation and conditioning. I say to you, I proclaim to you: "The ENDS NEVER justify the means." Whenever you "feel" you are in that situation, you are being asked to commit to a "Devil's Bargain." Your ONLY POWR IS YOUR REFUSAL. We can make the world beautiful again. We can make the world peaceful for ONCE. We can provide for each person's ESSENTIAL NEEDS but we can't do it by using the SAME METHODOLOGY that has kept us ENTRENCHED IN A WAR OF INEQUALITY.

Day 1:

Wisdom of Silence:

"Give 'em Hell Boys!" becomes "Give 'em the Silent Treatment WOMEN, GIRLS, and ALL THE MEN WHO LOVE THEM!"

Problem is Native Americans haven't had a CHANCE to LEAD—neither have women or the descendents of Slaves. America was built by SLAVERY (and ALL its iterations—for the reality and practice may chance appearance as if a Chameleon but the Spirit remains and profligates) on the backs of slaves commercial

Wisdom of the Starter Story, the Three-Legged Stool & Three-Legged Race:

After attending graduate school in the Midwest and making a Patrilocal move of my family, I discovered the "bad" side of my in-laws pretty 1950s-era town. The "bad" side was where the "bad" store was where people who didn't have checking accounts could "cash" their paychecks "for a percentage cut" and a store that sold "expired" foods from "the back of the store." My own family's poverty had "forced" me (the middleclass but fallen into poverty from disease/disability, white, Christian woman) to become, circumstantially, "bad" but if I hadn't have been BROUGHT DOWN…I would never have met HER. She had bad teeth—most did. I assumed drugs but life would teach me the ERROR of that assumption as my own teeth became "bad" from the fact that there just wasn't ENOUGH MONEY for me to go to the dentist when my children and disabled husband needed to as well (Children and the disabled MUST ALWAYS GO FIRST). So I noticed her bad teeth. I made assumptions (most likely erroneous) but I also like talking to people—learning their stories—so we began to chat while I paid for day-old bread and expired frozen catfish. She told me that she was a writer and that she made money at it. Of course I was interested. I still believed I was middleclass—and educated—so, naturally, I wanted MY writing to MAKE money too. I was all enthusiastic Ear. She told me that she made $50 from a company for her "Starter" stories. I'd never heard of such a thing. She kindly explained that she develops the characters, plot, and setting but doesn't have to write the whole thing—just the basics—the "skeleton." I remember being HORRIFIED that her creative ideas were being sold for $50. She must have seen an expression on my face that made her, quickly try to COMFORT ME, by saying, "I've got a million ideas. They come easy for me." And I shared with her the Wisdom of a Bodybuilder: nothing lasts forever and your creativity is a force of energy just like your body's force of energy…it, in youth, is perceived to be infinitely indefatigable but perception is not necessarily Truth. One day you will not be able to create stories so easily…like bending the knee…and one day, from there, you will not be able to create even a single word with which to BEGIN a story." She said, "I need the money." I said, "Then I'm so thankful your creativity can give you what you need. I'm just sorry it's not more than $50. It's worth SO MUCH MORE…and so are you."

The Wisdom of the Three-Legged Stool:

The three-legged stool of my Childhood milking days and of my Crone heart failure days let me see that the STABILITY NEEDED for FUNCTIONAL WORK relies on the STABILITY OF THE THREE LEGS IT RELIES/DEPENDS UPON; the same is true of our Society's "three-legged stool"…we just have to realize that being but ONE leg is JUST AS POWERFUL, functionally, as the SEAT upon which Industry rests its Fat Ass upon while exploiting the Maternal product of a Milked Cow. If ONE LEG wobbles, the WHOLE wobbles. Now a GOOD Farmer (as dairy "farmers" are not ranchers…they don't have to kill to exploit), though it's inconvenient and might interfere with the "plans of the day" they will, UPON NOTICING THE WOBBLE, finish their CURRENT MILKING (while having to put in greater effort/energy to ACCOMMODATE THE WOBBLE WHILE DOING THE SAME WORK), they will INSPECT the stool and DETERMINE (no matter how long it takes or how much EFFORT it takes) to FIND THE SOURCE OF THE WOBBLE—and then they will REPAIR IT because they, out of self-interest, understand that AN OUNCE OF PREVENTION IS WORTH A POUND OF CURE! The "bad" dairy farmer pays an illegal immigrant to suffer a wobbly stool, threatening them with either starvation (lost wage) or deportation (for many, starvation and/or death) if they don't KEEP UP THE MILKING PACE AS IF THEY ARE SITTING ATOP A FUNCTIONAL STOOL because they have determined that preventing a "poor" person's unnecessary suffering is NOT worth the OUNCE—for they KNOW they will never, not for the

Stranger, be REQUIRED TO PAY THE POUND—this is but the Chameleon's different MASK hiding the Spirit of Slavery we have yet to Overcome.

Wisdom of the Three-Legged Race

When I was in elementary school my very favorite school day in the world was National Child Health Day which we celebrated by having the afternoon to compete, physically, like potato sack race, raw egg toss, and the three-legged race where "rubber band" (pieces cut from tire inner-tubes). I've always been physically strong; stronger than most of the boys I went to school with even after puberty but I learned a valuable "lesson" specifically from one specific Three-Legged race. My best friend at the time was the daughter of a physician so, of course, we "paired" up. Now I can tell you that in addition to being physically strong I was also fiercely competitive; I could accept "losing" only if I'd given EVERYTHING I HAD and, in the three-legged race model, you can probably already predict this did not go so well. My doctor's daughter friend "quit" about halfway down the stretch. At first I tried cheerleader. It didn't work. Then I tried drill sergeant (being the daughter of a Marine I was well-versed) and this DEFINITELY didn't work…so I, literally, grabbed her so hard to my side that I "carried" her across the finish line—and we LOST…and I knew DAMNED WELL that if she hadn't have given up…we wouldn't have. I was PISSED! Needless to say, we were not friends for long afterwards.

As a Crone I see all of that differently—for how much better a friend would I have been if, when she'd reached her limit, I simply—out of LOVE FOR HER—stopped WITH her. I understand fierce competition and rigid intolerance—I have lived it…and I, as a Survivor, tell you—that is the path of Destruction and Sorrow.

But the Three-Legged Race (as with all dualities like blessing | curse) offers now—because of my own changed worldview—a DIFFERENT UNDERSTANDING OF THE SAME EVENT. I see the "binding" as a WAY TO HEAL (there's a reason why its medically referred to as "binding of wounds"—because even our blood and bone, when in close proximity, heal…but if too disconnected become necrotic—they Die and must be AMPUTATED or the spread of Death kills the ENTIRE ORGANISM.)

So let's create a Vision of a New World—let's REQUIRE "MARRIAGE" for our elected officials.

YOUTH: let the YOUTH LEAD but through the EXERCISE of "teamwork" as in the "THREE-LEGGED RACE" where, incrementally, each is "bound" to its opposite. So a 16 year old senator is "conjoined" with a 76 year old senator—both with EQUAL VOTING POWER so that, at worst, their "collective" vote is nullified (welcome to "normal" functioning of Congress is 2020 already between R & D). At least this way the two "Oppositional" ages will have to work together if they want to "win" the "Race."

People of color "bound" in their legislative POWER to whites. People of female biology "bound" in their legislative POWER to people of male biology. People of religious conviction "bound" to people of DIFFERING religious conviction (including the lack of religious conviction at all).

As far as I can see the system is broken because we've successfully "categorized and catalogued" our "species"—we really ARE good scientists—but what this Time of Trouble is calling for ALL OF US TO ACHIEVE is to reject the efficiency of science for the Wisdom of Human Connection.

The "binding" of which I speak is modeled after the Amish "Bundling" (or Tarrying) ritual—where a young couple is allowed to "sleep" together with a, literal, board between them (a physical barrier I'd suspect is as "effective" as any physical barrier—like a Wall) to "prevent" inappropriate LEVELS of intimacy/bonding (ie sex).

"Bundling" works if for nothing else but creating a measurable and physical opportunity for "intimacy." I'm sure there are "couples" who go to "bed" one night and are coupled no longer afterward for having spent 8 hours "being together without external distraction or influence."

I'd argue that the POWERFUL (ie white, old, rich, specifically Christian) NEED TO BE BUNDELED with their "opposition" (people of color, young, poor, any worldview other than Christian) if they want to experience the INTIMACY NEEDED for EVERYONE to be able to Survive.

Without this Marriage I fear the Schisms will prove insurmountable and, as ALWAYS, it will be ALL OF the CHILDREN who SUFFER for OUR *ABJECT* Failure! I pray we all do the Right thing. It would be nice if everyone did the right thing simply because it's the Right thing to do (but that's about the individual person's journey, not my circus—not my Monkey) but I PRAY everyone does the Right thing (stops, drops, and ROLLS, VIGOROUSLY) because we're SELF-IMMOLATING and I fear that our failure to ACT, swiftly and decisively, in this moment will be the Destruction of US (of All).

~~~

Chapter Omega

In this time there is nothing of greater value than an effective algorithm. There is no wealth or power without it.

The world needs one, true algorithm for the created hell on earth to be remedied. Unfortunately for the ego of mankind, as with Babylon, in God's wisdom He has entrusted each religion and philosophy with only one element of the algorithm and, if we are to remediate our hellish world we must come together, forcing all people to practice radical tolerance, to practice genuine listening to those willing to authentically and honestly speak, to practice radical love by loving something greater than oneself (even if that something greater is simply the Earth and this singular experience of it) and only then, through great self-discipline to counter our own egotism, can we begin.

THE GREAT FORUM

Each segment of society must be represented by not just one leader but by leaders of conflicting views within their own segment of society; this allows for the middle way.

Each segment of society must be represented; there is no stone that can be missing for that will prove a missing segment of the algorithm thereby rendering the algorithm nonfunctional—to exclude any segment is to render the entire hope for our Earth futile…hopeless.

There must be representation from all of the, approximately, 4,300 world religions including, but not limited to, Christian, Muslim, Jewish, Buddhist, Hindu, Taoist, Confucius, Wiccan, as well as all world Indigenous belief systems, as well as world religions as well as representatives from all world philosophies outside of the aforementioned religions including, but not limited to, Atheists, rationalist, objectivist, naturalists which may include: scientists, mathematicians, psychologists, sociologist, anthropologists, economists, political scientists, attorneys, judges, police, soldiers, etc who do not subscribe, ideologically, to anything more than the perfunctory.

Additionally, every societal segment group must include representatives across the socioeconomic classes within their own system and there must be parity, in terms of representation, of men, women, children, the aged, and the ill/disabled.

This forum is not meant to be easy. It is not meant to be comfortable or reassuring. It's meant to enable each of us to see the truth—the truth as seen through each set of eyes that have very different experience and understanding.

It is in through this cognitive dissonance, while practicing radical tolerance and radical love, that will enable us to have the greatest chance of uncovering the algorithmic elements each holds of piece of. We are being called to overcome Babylon and it is possible—but really fucking difficult and requires each representative to fight their own desire to lead, to rule, to enforce, to self-validate, and to embrace, genuinely and holistically, humility, humbleness, and the respect for all others as we'd have them respect us.

Our world has cancer. It is dying. It has been for a long time now. People sense it. People have to make "devil's bargains" just to survive. This path leads to destruction and death.

There is only one way to save our planet and ourselves: love. There is only one philosophy that can save the planet: do, say, and believe only what is good, right, beautiful, generous, tolerant, empathetic, sympathetic—your being cannot hold those things at its core while also accepting hatred, violence, greed, and corruption.

Now is the time for all the people of the world to decide—each of you have exactly the same power as anyone else—whether you are tired of that gnawing feeling that things aren't right (even our own personal choices) but that you are helpless to do anything about it, the lie, or choose to live lives of love for all life, not just in this moment but from this moment until the end of life.

Your power is your refusal.

From here I will speak from my own belief to my fellow Christian brothers and sisters:

One can be imprisoned—so be it. Many are in prison (even more in prisons without walls or the conditioned mind); if one is imprisoned for doing or believing what is good, upright, loving, and kind then who am I to believe I deserve to be treated differently?

One can be persecuted—so be it. Many are persecuted (even more in their own conditioned minds); if one is persecuted for doing or believing what is good, upright, loving, and kind then who am I to believe I deserve anything less?

One can be tortured—so be it. Many are tortured (even in their own conditioned minds); if one is tortured for doing or believing what is good, upright, loving and kind then who am I to believe I deserve not to be tortured?

One can be oppressed—so be it. Many are oppressed (both physically and by their own conditioned mind); if one is oppressed for doing or believing what is good, upright, loving and kind then who am I to believe I deserve freedom, privilege, and authority?

One can be murdered—so be it. There is nothing more common in this world.

But I say to you, of my own belief, that those who love their lives will lose them, that the last will be first and the first will be last, and—most importantly—God love the world…and His heart is breaking for the choices we are making. Do not lie, Do not steal, Do not covet, Do not…there are too many of us that can recite the rules…but we have completely misunderstood the God News of our Savior—Jesus Christ who gave us just TWO LAWS: 1) love God first and most and 2) love each other as I have loved you.

You MUST ponder Christ's radical vision of a world filled with his love. You MUST use your imagination not on fantasies about conquest and worldly heroism but to envision the world Christ meant for us to realize through the PRACTICING (in all aspects of our lives ranging from the interpersonal to the international) of Christ's LOVE.

Christ came as the prescription to heal the sickness of the world (which was shown to us, vividly, in the Old Testament. It is filled with terror and all manners of disgusting corruption—and there is not one single human behavior accounted for in the Old Testament that is not now—in 2019—still happening in the world in spite of Christ providing the cure more than 2,000 years ago.

The time is running out. You Christians, who don't want to give up worldly power, are soon to be left to your own devices; the "Sermon-on-the-Mount" Christians are coming to an end. You have mistakenly believed that the rapture will save you from the suffering that is to come, that you who go to church but will not refuse to work for an employer who is corrupt or whose practices are not loving, kind, generous, and produce good fruits (fruits that provide to all the groups of people Christ so loved, including widows, orphans, the poor, the sick, the mentally ill, the physically disabled, the hungry, the weak, the "dregs" of society including the whores, the addicts) then you are not fulfilling the heart of Christ.

I can only imagine that almost every Christian who reads this will automatically decry me as idealistic, unrealistic, childish, zealot, there are so many synonyms, but I am only speaking your own Savior's words to you; if it is repulsive to you or does not feel comfortable to you…then I would suggest you explore your own heart and mind.

The two commandments of Christ are not easy to follow but neither are they impossible. It requires us, as Christians, to make the world know us not as those wielding swords or negating God's own establishment of Choice (Free will was instituted by God, who created ALL things, including good and evil so that we COULD have the free will to exercise choice). Those who would seek to "prevent" anyone from anything are directly defying the divine right of God to establish, in this world, that it is His authority alone to judge how we, as individuals, have lived our own individual lives.

To deny a person the choice for good or evil is to deny the first authority God established for man in the Garden of Eden: temptation and the choice either to yield to or refuse it.

So, again, our ONLY POWER, is our refusal. It is a crime against God to deny any other person the right to choose. We are not each other's parent (only God is) but we are each other's keeper, thus Christ's prescription for how to cure our world's cancer and heal the world in order that we may care for each other, all our brothers and sisters around the world, as Christ has cared (and still cares) for us.

I pray for this radical transformation of America—so that it can become what it was meant to be: the Shining City on the Hill, a beacon of hope, a land ruled through love and kindness and available to all who seek such love, during this Second Crucifixion of Christ's Body (or the established Church of Christ).

I pray in the name of the Father, the Son, and the Holy Spirit.

May God bless and keep you all, today and always.

~~~

He knew that the Church would have no choice but to react; it had long since granted its fealty to the World. Shortly after its dissemination, the Preacher was informed that he would be transferred just once more. To a Fortaleezian parish in the middle of nowhere. The Church assured him, in writing, that the traditional debt requirement for enrollment in the Fortaleezian program had been waived, permanently, so there was no need for him to ever worry about the provision of his needs: he would never be without food, shelter, water, healthcare, and meaningful work.

The Preacher had been given Wisdom to discern Truth from Deception. He could filter out the manipulation and lies which allowed him to resist the Church's temptation that spoke only to his flesh. He knew their hearts in spite of Silver Tongues and Schemes. The intent was to relegate him to obscurity. To kill his voice in its crib.

What they, in their inability to hear, to recognize, or to understand Truth (which, like vampires to sunlight, not only repulses them but injures) fail to comprehend is that it is always...will always be...God's will...not theirs—unless their will aligns with the Queen Mother Bride of Christ.

What they fail to understand is that they send me to Fortaleez to disconnect the call from God that is—that has always been—intended for THEM...and God, though patient and enduring, will not remain so...forever. So where I go, therefore go God's seed—for I, too, now am Christ's Bride. I have extracted my own heart, I have killed myself in my own spirit, so that I may have my donor's, Christ's, patchwork inside me no differently than the world's Frankenstein...but where man serves to create its monsters—the King and Queen make Peaceful Love.

Their plan will fail because, deep inside, the last remnant breathe of God inside each soul...is dying...and we—conscious of it or not—feel Death's exertion inside. Everyone knows, at some level, that this is not how we're supposed to be living: God's Wisdom through Christ's Love create the two-parted navigational tool needed to come through these dark seas—but without the Spirit of Christ indwelled—as evidenced by one's actions not words—then we will ALL be lost to the Deep. We are, cosmically and physically, bound to each other—the Mothers and the Fathers. Our fates are interdependent. And our Maker, our Creator, has provided a Way...and it is radical: do the right thing because it is the right thing to do. Do all things lovingly because it is the right thing to do. Be kind, patient, generous, self-less (which is not the same as codependent), and always give everyone the benefit of the doubt—to trust—until given reason not to, which requires the utmost diligence for each other as brothers and sisters. And attend to every grievance with the involved parties, with loving and wise mediation if the dispute is intractable, before ANYTHING else. Grievance unaddressed and unresolved is the Path to

Destruction. So is lying and deceit so never, NEVER EVER, bear or deliver false witness: we must always, ALWAYS, tell the truth, the whole truth, and nothing but the Truth, so help us God. Amen.

The Gift I leave to you is the Heart of Christ Rosary Prayer. May the meditative focus serve you as well as it has served me; I created a sculpture to help me focus on the Truth—you will find what best suits you as a tool…how, the method by which one focuses energy and effort matters nothing but the intention—the focus OF your energy—matters more than anything. I created art to help me focus. You will have different methods but, together, in proper focus and intention we will make the world become God's image for His Bride's fantasy for the world he envisioned but we have failed to realize. In fact, I'd testify today, that we humans have all but given up the Ghost for our focus is as far from God's as Mars is from our grasp. Your brother Christ, 11/25/2019 2:38:09 PM

The Heart of Christ Rosary Meditative Prayer:

I.   Preparatory Introduction:

I.	II.	III.	IV.	V.	VI.	VII.	
Hold the Cross. Breathe in fully. Focus on Love. Exhale fully	Hold the Cross. Breathe in fully. Focus on Peace. Exhale fully	Hold the Cross. Breathe in fully. Focus on Tolerance. Exhale fully	Hold the Cross. Breathe in fully. Focus on Generosity. Breathe out fully	Hold the Lone Bead. Recite, aloud, Christ's two laws/Commands: 1) Love God first; and 2) Love each other as I (Christ) have loved You.	With Care, hold each of the following 3 Beads: Breathe in deeply With each. Reflect on the wisdom of the Mothers With Each Bead. Breathe out deeply	On the Lone Bead Breathe in deeply. Reflect on the wisdom of the Fathers Breathe out deeply ~~~ Journey to the Metal. Hold the Metal. Ponder, Carefully,	You have completed Proper Introduction Etiquette. ~~~ Now begin the Decades Of Meditation.

						The Proper & Improper Uses of *ALL* Metal.	

II.   The Disciple's Refocused Intention

Now Begin the Decades, or the Becoming (The five groupings of ten beads represent the tangible action and soulful commitment in preparation to practice, without fail, Jubilee).

The Decades of Meditation	I.	II.	III.	IV.	V.	VI.	VII.	VIII.	IX.	X.	On the large bead Revel
Breathe in and out, naturally & completely, contemplating each bead.	Beads 1-6: Consider a single sorrow of another. Beads 7-9: Consider three sorrows, focusing on a single sorrow with each bead, from the World God loves. Bead 10: Consider a single sorrow of your own for this is a Healing	Beads 1-6: Consider a single sorrow of another. Beads 7-9: Consider three sorrows, focusing on a single sorrow with each bead, from the World God loves. Bead 10: Consider a single sorrow of your own for this is a Healing	Beads 1-6: Consider a single sorrow of another. Beads 7-9: Consider three sorrows, focusing on a single sorrow with each bead, from the World God loves. Bead 10: Consider a single sorrow of your own for this is a Healing	"	"	"	"	"	"	"	Wisdom and Joy Are Sabbatical and Jubilee. Repeat the Decades until the 50th bead. Then Begin The Closing

	(Golden) Ratio.	(Golden) Ratio.	(Golden) Ratio.				

III.   The Closing in Hopes of Renewed Rightness/Righteousness

I.	II.	III.	IV.	V.	VI.	VII.	VIII.
Contemplate the Permanence & Impermanence of **_ALL_** Metal As it both Begins & Ends The Decades.	On the Lone Bead: Breathe in deeply. Reflect on the wisdom of the Fathers. Breathe out deeply	On the next 3 beads (note: also a Healing Ratio): Breathe in deeply. Reflect on the wisdom of the Mothers. Breathe out deeply	Hold _the_ Lone Bead. Breathe Naturally. Recite, aloud, Christ's two laws/Commands: 1) Love God first; and 2) Love each other as I (Christ) have loved You.	Hold the Cross. Breathe in fully. Focus on Generosity. Breathe out fully	Hold the Cross. Breathe in fully. Focus on Tolerance. Exhale fully	Hold the Cross. Breathe in fully. Focus on Peace. Exhale fully	Hold the Cross. Breathe in fully. Focus on Love. Exhale fully

WISDOM of the Heart of Christ Rosary Meditative Prayer:

If you do this as often as you exercise and feed your body, with as much focus and intention, then you will begin to notice how some things are easier for you to either consider and/or remember.

Some things come more naturally than others—those are your natural tendencies, either for restriction or indulgence—but it is the ones that prove elusive or pesky, the ones you grow frustrated with because they indicate (like the lights on your dashboard) where something is not working well…the Wisdom of this Disciplined Approach (which is only one way of approach but as with ALL ways…this will help some grow closer to Wisdom; others will find better ways for them to achieve the same goal—to Heal Ourselves…as the World's Sorrow is from Our ABUSE of all that inhabit it, including ourselves, but as we—humans—are the ones with consciousness then the responsibility to rise to whatever occasion calls us to service.

Time is Calling to the Deep: We all must choose how and if we answer, as individuals, and—as individuals—our choices for our actions will be counted. Amen my fellow humanitarians. May we, through our actions, fulfill our Sacred Duty to Fulfill and make Manifest the Sacred Heart of Christ through outward and unfailing displays of Love, Peace, Tolerance, and Generosity as this is the Edict of Christ's Commands.

NON-EPHEMERAL MODIFICATION OF PRACTICE:

The practice of the Heart of Christ Rosary is ONE way for ME to focus on others more than myself, to focus on BOTH the forest AND the trees (not binaries), and to ATTEMPT to connect my heart and mind to ALL life on Earth through ACTION not words.

But I am conditioned to seek understanding through my faith and culture and this means what "works" for me—the details and bobbles—will not work for Many, especially those with different faith and culture but the "details" (perhaps trigger "words and phrases") are but bobbles!

The practice is Gold, Silver, Platinum, and Diamond.

So for those who can't stomach the Rosary, don't. But don't let whatever makes your stomach reject the "bobble" rob you of the treasure rightfully yours: the practice.

For me, this understanding came after I'd practiced the Heart of Christ Rosary enough that I didn't have to "concentrate" on the Practice, which allowed me to "experience" the lesson for me to learn: I began searching the Rosary's focuses in the "real" world of Social Media.

So I'd search for "Love" in the news, scrolling through the posts, for at least three consecutive pages, breathing and focusing on each. I'd search "Peace," "Generosity" and "Tolerance" while remaining in the same attitude.

When I was done with this "homework" then I'd take however much time and energy I had in reserve and I'd focus on my personal relationship, to myself and to others and to the Earth, and try to "relate" to whatever/whoever else I'd seen—the posts—of what was the core tenets of my faith: love, peace, generosity, and tolerance.

Through this practice I found myself "feeling" (heart and mind) greater connection to others, the Earth, and myself—without indulging the conditioned aspects of my personal culture and faith.

I share this with you as it was of help to me—and as we are never as unique as we like to believe—I imagine there might be at least one other person on the planet that might find this of value as well. Amen.

~~~

Author Notes by K.A. Shott:

(Note: The Preacher is personified via written method creation technique modeled after Konstantin Sergeievich Stanislavski's method acting for Russian theater [1930s].)

The Preacher's Prophesy began 11/25/2020

My Skeletal began 11/26/2020

My Genesis of fictional text begun: 5/8/2020

Changed Title (major directional focus shift) 6/1/2020 from (The Optimistic American Book III: Judgment & Sentencing By K.A. Shott but voiced through the character of The Preacher (Evangelissimo)) to "PREACH" by K.A. Shott

06.14.2020 completed first draft (46942 words/106 pages); Preach is a trance-state movement meditation (my first attempt at using my 'language' of choice—the written aspect of Commune—to observe and interact with 'my' mind. I attempted, as best I could, to be completely honest and unfiltered. At first a word came to me, "Closer," but as Preach progressed the word "Disambiguation," replaced it; at times I wondered if I'd gone insane/crazy—so I preface whatever meaning you might draw from Preach to consider the reliability of its source (Voir Dire); I will (like *The Joker*) insert a caveat: in a world that, to my eyes looks entirely insane with a psychopathic/sociopathic diagnosis—I'd suggest that my "variant" of "insanity" is more of a "retardation" or "regression" to the mind of a child…I realize that both variations are "crazy" but I'd prefer an adult with the mind of a child over a psychotic killer skilled in manipulation and deception. Stylistically, Preach celebrates the spirit of the Impressionists by embracing and incorporating the BIRTH OF A BRAND NEW LANGUAGE STYLE (the BIGsmall case of YelLinG language) and just as in the past, innovation is made fun of until it becomes fully assimilated (just ask Vincent van Gogh) but Preach also honors the NaNoWriMo challenge—for it was generated, beginning to end, in 37 days; I acknowledge that this is 7 days longer than the Annual 30-day writing challenge but it was the best I could do (especially while incorporating a new language). The final mantra of Preach came today, 06.15.2020, as Schoolhouse Rock's refrain from the song, *The British are Coming! The British are Coming*! "And the *shot* heard 'round the world was the start of the Revolution."

06.18.2020 Contemplated and discussed merger of "Preach" with "Ideal" in one book (the twins birthed) for it is right but it is also the last time Max and I will be able to use the Method so it felt like the honorable thing to do, for him and for me, to approach this last endeavor with the respect and appreciation that comes from acknowledging the ending of an Era; the book size (10x 13 v 6x9) will allow real scale of cover art (watercolor with mathematic "opposite" sign between titles Preach and Ideal on top and bottom illustrating that the art can be approached from every aspect/angle with equal degree of different understanding/meaning—it is titled, from one aspect, "f(x)=1/x; asymptote" and from the opposite aspect titled, "Force Coupling" both aspects labeled, "Preach = Ideal" but with the Opposite Sign between them (instead of what is available on the keyboard [=]) at the "top" depending on one's orientation.ly but differently.

06.22.2020 Four days of keeping company with a discomforting sense that I was not handling *Preach* or *Ideal* Correctly. After watching the Poor People's Protest 06.20.2020 and Pope Francis's address of Congress in 2015 I felt convicted that *Preach* had to be published "As Is" because it is an Exercise in Trusting God. I confess that I Craved applying the process Max and I had always done with our other projects for it was a Coupling Bond. I confess that I was excited, as I held the manuscript in one hand and pen in the other, reading aloud while making slash marks—like a wildfire forest firefighter—because there is something gratifying about cutting away, pruning, forming; as if words are to become clay-formed Golem. It took more than twenty pages before that Gnawing Feeling reached my fingers and felled my pen. For with each stroke I was denying, like Paul, the Spirit which had deemed me a Worthy Vessel and even though I'd done my best to be Humble, trusting God and the Holy Spirit of Christ throughout the Genesis, once there was a Product that would enter the Market—I became "afraid" or rather my Hubris—like a drunk Uncle or Abusive Father—grabbed God's Gifts from His Extended Hand; my Hubris has a hard time surrendering Control. To publish something sight-unseen is terrifying because I KNOW how shitty my unadulterated writing is—and THIS TWINNED project (*Preach* and *Ideal*) are the most important things I'll ever write and, in MY mind, that means they need to be the MOST Perfected by MY hand. Wrong. *Preach* is not important because of the words written on the page…it is MOST IMPORTANT because it is my Display of Faith. I trust that God will do whatever He wants or needs with regard to Every Thing connected to "my" Life. That is what *Preach* is. A Trust Fall—and I KNOW, with every atom in the Universe of Me, that God will Catch me in exactly the way I must be Caught—for His Hands are THE ONLY Hands I Need. Through this facing of Fear, of rejecting Anxiety, of Trusting in something Great, and Surrendering the Outcome—I find Peace, Love, Generosity, and Tolerance within myself. It is the beginning step of a thousand steps. For if I can experience such things within—I pray, through a lifetime spent in such Attitude, such experience can become without. Amen.

www.ingramcontent.com/pod-product-compliance
Lightning Source LLC
Chambersburg PA
CBHW081205170626
46813CB00010B/3330